THE OPEN
MON

five stories se

CW01669303

In *On the Bent and Narrow* Son
conversion on the road to salvation after a tragedy has him reassessing his life of lying and greed. Sonny first touted for business in Paul Mann's *The Park Job* published by Gay Men's Press. "*The Park Job*...is most memorable..." ~ *Gay Reporter*

In *The Open Season for Mongooses* Jacob collars a conman while being taken for a ride by the conman's protégé. This story links to Paul Mann's acclaimed adventure novel *Nailing Frank*. *Nailing Frank* was presented by the UK Equalities Minister, Maria Eagle, as a Cultural Award to Kyrgyzstan LGBT.

In *The Office Boy* a close and tender friendship develops between nineteen year old Boyd and middle aged Simon. This is a revised version of the story first published by Third House in *Fabulous Tricks*.

Looking for Something on an unusual evening out in Brighton.

JUMP!

More veterans have committed suicide since the Falklands War than died in the conflict

Civilian life has Ralph in an office where many letch after the ex-marine. Ralph relives a terrorist incident in Lebanon and active service in the Falklands where the injured were often too damaged to be shown on television. Their images on screen would restrain the flag-waving *Land of Hope and Glory* crowds when the ships returned to the UK. A parachute instructor reckons Ralph is suffering from Post Traumatic Stress Disorder. Therapy is to get Ralph to jump again.

Paul Mann is a member of
Royal Marines 42 Commando Association

Also by Paul Mann

The Queer Commando
The Seaman's Mission
Nailing Frank
Stowaway
The Last Cargo Ship
The Queer Businessman

THE OPEN SEASON

FOR

MONGOOSES

Paul Mann

Paradise Press
London

Published in association with Paradise North 2014
by
Paradise Press
B M Box 5700
London WC1N 3XX

British Library Cataloguing in Publication Data.
A catalogue record for this book is available from the British Library.

The original painting on the cover shows the author, hands in pockets, under the GENTS sign.

ISBN 978-1-904585-42-8

Contents

THE OPEN SEASON FOR MONGOOSES

On the chain ferry, that clanked its way across Poole Harbour's narrow mouth, many of my fellow passengers I knew from the pub. Puff, young and froufrou and friendly with a bleached hearthrug of hair, talked to the nice balding guy I chat to some evenings. But not looking me in the eye was the camp Scotsman with whom I had spent an afternoon in his room in Poole.

Three minutes and we were at Shell Bay.

Getting in the way of the twenty-four cars that bumped down the ramp were the Mateus Rosé Quartet flying high; one carried the wine, another sported an opened transparent plastic umbrella on a cloudless day; he patted me alcoholically on my shoulder. "We're down for the weekend again. See you on the beach?"

Not the packed beach at Shell Bay where children shrieked and youths tough-kicked a football and a painfully pink toddler played with a plastic spade at the water's edge. All the holidaymakers herded together. Shell Bay was their place.

I cycled past two portaloos acrid in the sun, past a first-aid post with an on duty bare-chested, jeans-wearing macho man. And well before Studland village I turned off the asphalt road and slung my bike in bushes and took a rough path busy with dragon flies and midges. Then pushing through squelchy marsh and reeds I braved the African Queen crossing to reach The Colony.

The Colony was a peaceful enclave maybe a half a mile

long and of similar width; there was thin wood at the marsh end, and grass-topped sand dunes formed its southern boundary; beyond was the sea. The Colony was a refuge from caring mums, from families, from fun. It was a serious place in which to hunt. The heather was pocked with dish shaped burrows, many occupied by naturists – all male. Periodically a naturist would pop up and inspect the landscape like a mongoose. But these mongooses were not only keeping a keen lookout but checking out the action.

One stood advertising himself. He left his burrow to walk The Colony and look at others. Walk. Look. Examine. This was a prelude to sex.

I waved to a waiter from Florida on vacation and to the laboratory assistant from Yorkshire who had varicose veins and was on his annual pilgrimage. I stuck up two fingers at Jim, the grinning hall porter from my hotel, and headed for the Resident Elder who camped out nights – tentwise – and wore frilly powder blue knickers. His hair was bleached to straw and his chest and stomach were shaved. With his transistor blasting pop he talked of the silence at dawn when the deer came close to his tent and last night an adder had slithered in and curled up near his sleeping bag. "When I woke it had gone," he said with regret. The Resident Elder sat, where he usually sat, on broken concrete slabs; all that remained of the Wartime observation post.

"Trippers!" he said, speaking with a contempt he reserved for politicians. "Trippers! We had an *invasion,* my dear. Two sunbathed and embraced, pecking and kissing." He pointed to the spot where they had been. "There! Heterosexuals!"

I said, "Met one couple. The husband was gorgeous and

into sex with me. The wife wanted only to watch. I felt I did my bit to keep their marriage together."

I then headed for my favourite sandy hollow from where I watched a hugely fat middle-aged man trailed by an exotic young man. I ducked down and pretended to read my paperback.

The stillness about me was broken by a rustle, the tall young man with the magic touch of the East sat on haunches, watching me, innocent, smiling.

"I'm Frank. You are?"

"Jacob. You're a marvellous colour – you make the British seem insipid."

"I am from Lancashire. My father was Romany."

We talked for an hour and he asked if I had a place to go as he never did it in the sand. I shook my head, thinking this lad with his strong Lancastrian accent would be intimidated by my hotel.

"*The Club Reef* tonight," he said, kissing me gently on the lips.

"Never been there."

"Don't make it too late."

In *The Club Reef* the doorman, with highlighted hair, bolted the door behind me. And in a delicious way – as though the club were a speakeasy about to be raided – said, "You do know this is gay?"

"If I look straight, head me towards the nearest lipstick – carmine for choice."

"Borrow my Blushing Pink." His arm was hooked in mine as he led me to a balustrade from where we looked down on the bar and a patch of dance floor.

There was a Chinese, skinny as a filleted pencil,

wearing hideous round spectacles talking to a macho man in tight jeans who had his startling black hairy chest on display. And one guy hitting six-five, was wearing a warm tweed jacket with cavalry twills, and looked as though he had left his horse outside.

"A somewhat mixed clientèle?" I said.

"You don't reckon the muscle man?"

"Him with the tattoos?"

"No, Muscles Two sipping a Campari soda. He speaks soprano," the doorman pointed at a guy whose torso was exploding out of a snow white vest.

"Impressive," I said.

"He camouflages his femininity with muscles manufactured in the gym," he said.

"Love the Bisto tan."

"Makeup."

"By Meow?" I said, "Trouble is the poor soul didn't know when to call time. Everywhere is bursting at the seams."

"There too. What he's got between his legs is a crowd puller but he don't pull it, only pierce it and piss through it. Seen him in an Amsterdam sauna, face down, serving the Common Market."

"I'm looking for Frank?"

"Frank ain't for you, Jacob."

"How'd you know my name? I'm not wearing my name-tag-in-case-I-get-lost-in-Queersville, am I?"

"You've got style, Carmine Lippy, and you've got a friend – Jim – from your hotel who is looking out for you. Said you'd smooth in. He's gone back on duty. Set you up with Trev?" The doorman nodded towards a slim fair haired guy, early twenties maybe, sipping Cokes. Suede shoes and a kind of nice shy look.

"Yeah?"

"Surprisingly normal. Don't get them too often in here. Oh, a proviso, he's scared of cats," he said.

"I'm meeting Frank."

"The cat-phobic guy's got the reliability factor. And he don't want nothing only a smile when you say goodbye."

He left me when the door buzzer sounded so I talked to the avoiding-cat-guy. Bought him a Coke, and was up front, told him I was looking for Frank.

"There's your man. Alongside the pillar."

Frank grasped my arm and dragged me to a table in a dark alcove; sat me down and towered over me. Face smooth and square, high cheek-bones, golden skin, hip-tight white jeans and a yellow body-hugging top.

"Don't you follow fashion?" he said, obviously appalled by my clothes. He whispered, "Do you have a car? We can get out of here and go to a hotel now."

Angrily defensive, I said, "No, I am one of the disabled in modern mobility. I bicycle."

"*Cycle*?" he said, as though I walked naked through the town. Then came the lecture. Hadn't been lectured since I was thrown out of school. Frank did a good job of looking down on me as had my late headmaster. "We are gay people. We have to attract others. You are dressed like a clerk." He glanced about presumably terrified that someone he knew would see him talking to dull unfashionable me.

I was sort of taken aback but fascinated by him but as he was as sexy as hell, and had suggested a hotel, I kept my temper, said, "You obsessed with clothes or something? My headmaster was. He went on about how he was grateful I no longer wore the school uniform when he kicked me out. And what's wrong with being a clerk?"

I had on a lightweight suit 'cos I was going to take him out to supper – in a taxi not slung over the crossbar of a Raleigh Rudge.

"See you on the beach sometime," was his brush off line.

I do better brush off lines but needed a drink like now and would not leave because that would be showing defeat and I don't do defeat as I explained to the guy who was afraid of cats and as we shared jokes he told me about his current infatuation after I had told him about mine.

I said, "Clubs aren't me at all. Last club I went to was with Dad."

"Gay?"

"Doubt it. But who knows? Loads of dead necked wankers – retired military men and boring old farts from the City – pickled in malt whisky served from cut glass decanters on silver trays. I saw two men wearing monocles. Unbelievable. *Guinness Book of Records* stuff? My father refused to allow me to take photographs of them. Hungry?"

"Wish you had asked like two hours ago. I've feasted on fish and chips."

"Fish is cat food. Is it all cats you hate?" I said.

"Don't hate them – cats scare me. Siamese give me the runs. You find that weird?"

"Nope. It's humans that move my bowels."

"I scare you?" he said.

"No, you're vulnerable. That's endearing. Sorry, I am hitting on you."

"I'm going your way. Want a lift?" He had long legs, a flop of silky light brown hair. Good features.

"How'd you know which way I am going?" I said.

"Highway 69 with the roadworks and exposed pipes?"

"You know Jim at the hotel?" I said.

"Jim handed me your résumé muttering, he's hot."

"Really? Jim scares me shitless. Young, self assured and has so much going for him I am erect as he goes by. I'm Jacob."

"Trev."

"How about a drink or ten at my hotel and we pick up samosas and a curry on the way? Or I can order something from room service? It's cat free and you can sleep it off. Twin beds if you baulk at the sight of me naked. You bothered if Jim is on duty?"

"God no. Jim and I go way back to primary school. Academically it was not a school of note. Sex education was not on the curriculum so Jim and I held midday classes for two in the woods, playing hooky and practising masturbation – see, we learnt a new word. Later on we did it as compulsory homework. Kind of set us up for liking each other long term." He grinned. "If Jim has got so much going for him maybe he and I should try it again? He's very obliging. I need practice. I'd say you don't?"

"If only. I get tongue tied or talk too much. Always at the wrong moment."

On our way out, I looked back, Frank was smooching on the dance floor with a fat man.

Trev said, "*That* is your competition? He's visual vomit. Called Smith and he name drops and bullshits like there is no tomorrow. Invited me back to his hotel – same hotel you stay. Said he was scouting for talent for TV. That was crap. He didn't know I work for one of the big theatrical agencies."

"I want your company, want you to come back, shoot the breeze, do whatever, do nothing if you don't like the view. I might cry but please don't turn nasty."

He laughed. “Jim was right, you’re okay.” Trev’s arm was reassuring in mine.

Trev had to work the next morning and as the day was overcast, the beach was out. Anthony, the hotel receptionist, was his usual facetious self, overdoing the sirs, holding onto my mail, holding my eyes.

“Sir, saw your breakfast companion. Trev had hot buttered toast and scrambled eggs. Gorged on chunky marmalade. Such an appetite. Did he…?”

“Did he what, Anthony?”

“Trev is annoyingly discreet – hate the bastard. Do you have something to tell me about his appetites?”

“He likes eggs.”

“You’re in jeans? Jim and I pray for you in shorts. I have a cable for you, sir? ETA FLORIDA OCTOBER FIRST STOP. Do you want me to ask for clarification?”

“No.”

“Are we a sailor, sir?”

“Barnacled to the back teeth. On board ship I drink Jamaican rum, smoke shag, sing sea shanties and when I play the hornpipe I dream of you.”

“I’d like that, sir.”

“Call me sir again and I will kill you, Anthony.”

“Aren’t we in demand today, sir? Another message from your father’s PA. You are to read yesterday’s *Financial Times*.”

“The ‘sirs’ aren’t funny.”

“I’ve had a copy of the *F.T.* sent up to your room, Jacob. Saw your dad’s photo in it. He is so cool.”

“Not for you unless the Lord Mayor’s banquet is your idea of a night of depravity. You’d like him. He said of

Thatcher that she cures the disease by killing the patient with it."

"I am into older men," said Anthony.

"Are you fluttering your ironic eyelashes at me?" I pushed my duffle bag at him. "You okay looking after it?"

"Jim said he saw you on the beach. Such a treat. Distingué even naked. No beach today? Are we not bicycling?"

I leant over the counter, my face close to his. "Shanks' pony."

"I wouldn't mind a ride," he whispered, at last making a move on me.

Face to face, so close I could smell his breath, see the sadness in his eyes. Neither of us was laughing.

"Sorry…" he said "…and hold the 'I like you but…' the 'buts' are the story of my life."

On Poole Quay the drizzling rain kept holidaymakers away but a few of the bored parked their cars at the edge of the quay and peered into grey mist. There was the smell of the sea and alongside was a Masefield coaster, its many rivets were thick coated with black paint, and weed floated below the Plimsoll line.

Stalwart sat the Resident Elder who had moved post from The Colony. Thankfully the blue frilly knickers were concealed beneath baggy denim. He shifted his large body along the bench to make room for me, gave me shelter beneath his golfing umbrella.

The Resident Elder addressed not only me but the seagulls. "Jacob, have you met someone?" The soaring gulls were losing interest, so he threw more bread. They shrieked, dived.

I told him of my liking for Frank and Frank's disgust at my clothes.

"Take him to your hotel?"

"It's too ostentatious for him," I said.

"Oh, my dear, one doubts that. I had a Romany friend once, be prepared for large genitals. I am now sharing my tent with a milkman. Blond and nice but he disappears dreadfully early as does the adder… Jacob, your wealth is showing."

"Who says I am wealthy?"

The Resident Elder studied me. "Your hotel screams it. Your white t-shirt with blue trimming contrasts expensively with your tan. You *could* be a deckhand off a Mediterranean yacht but when you open your mouth, I hear a fifteen thousand pound a year school."

"I…"

"Have you read the local paper? The most marvellous headline NUDITY SHOCKS AT NATURIST BEACH. Evidently a middle aged couple stumbled on two men 'kissing' and 'doing other things'."

"It's not dangerous, is it?"

"The police sometimes visit but are usually too busy pursuing real criminals."

The drizzle turned to heavy rain. Raindrops darkened my jeans.

The Resident Elder deserted me, saying, "I'm away to shelter in a delightful tearoom I know."

After lunch the sun was strong and the wind was drying so I asked the hall porter to rummage behind the reception desk for my duffle bag.

As he pushed my tip in his pocket, Jim said, "Shouldn't

take this. Seeing you naked is enough of a tip for me."

"Why do you and Anthony take the piss all the time?"

"Was fixing you up with Trev, taking the piss?"

"Trev's nice."

"Neither of you are after nice. You both are into disasters." Then Jim's manner became unusually solemn. "Jacob, you got a minute? Outside?"

Close to a high white wall, sheltering from the wind, Jim said that he knew Frank from the club.

"Got obsessed with him," I said.

"Last night that wanker was on about you dressing like a clerk according to what Trev said. I saw you, real sharp. I reckon that suit would cost me four month's wages."

"You checking up on me?" I said.

"Looking after you, mate."

"Try the suit on. Size-wise we're two peas in a pod. Might be tight in the crotch for you."

"You serious?" he said.

"I am but a simple sailor off to South America. On the estancias, it's denim and chaps. Take the fucking suit, Jim or I'll stick my tongue down your throat."

"I could treat Mum to dinner, wear it then?"

"Corned beef in Argentina?"

"Plaice and chips in the New Forest," he said.

"Make it turbot and that'll buy the wine." I tucked notes into his pocket.

"Piss off, Jacob! I fucking mean it."

"Stop your scoffing?"

"It's only 'cos I like you."

"I'm fighting back tears," I said. "Take it or I'll make a scene." I squeezed his balls.

That had Jim nervously looking about to see if anyone had seen us.

"Report me. I'll admit it," I said.

"Don't let on to Frank that you're staying here. If he knew, he'd be having sex with your wallet." Jim then asked the question which Anthony would never have asked. "What you doing living here for anyway?"

"Nowhere to go," I said.

"Why's that then?"

"You don't want to know."

"You've had sex with my best mate and we both kind of like you."

"You really don't want to know, James."

"But you need to tell me, Jacob. I can see your tears?"

"In April my brother shackled himself to a railway line. I identified the body. They gave me a large scotch before, and a much larger one after. Dad was in Japan. My mother celebrated the event by taking on another lover who is just out of nappies. I had to get rid the house – it's in the sticks and vulnerable to burglars so I got the contents into storage and leased the place. I've no home, Jim. Oh, there's a place in the country – can't stay there. Too many memories. We holidayed there as kids – me and Geoff."

I can't think about Geoff without the racking sobs, they still came in strong after four months. And poor Jim, tall and tough, had a worried frown. He soft-touched my cheek with his knuckles and this gentle contact had me following him. He was guiding me out of sight of the hotel entrance where he gave me a tissue. I think it had been used but his gesture made me even more emotional. It was a couple of minutes before I got under control.

"I'm over it. And I'm off. You don't deserve my shit."

"You want I get Jennie?" he said. Jennie was the chambermaid who cleaned my room.

"I'm okay."

"She'd want to?" said Jim.

I blew my nose into the tissue; pocketed it as if for support. "You wanted to warn me about Frank?"

"No, Frank ain't bad, there just ain't very much to him. All looks and fashion-clothes pimped from some guy. You all right now, Jacob?"

"So, this isn't about Frank?"

"His fat friend named Smith is the villain. Trev said he was at the club?"

"Yeah, must be like having sex with a water bed."

"That fat git is staying here and has accused one of the staff of nicking his wallet. A load of cash. Load of bollocks." Jim studied my face as he handed me a photo-copied hotel reservation card which recorded Smith's full name, his home address and other personal details. "You up to this?"

"Sure."

"Get someone to run a check on the fat man? And don't say where you got this from or I'll be out on my ear."

"Got you."

"You sure you're okay doing it?"

"I've known you for months and you picked me up when I was on my face in vomit in the drive. You carried me back, cleaned me up and patted my brow. And never said a word to anyone, not even Anthony. You can ask me to kiss your feet. Take off your shoes, I lust after your sweaty feet," I said.

"Not scoffing, Jennie reckons you," he said.

"When Jennie cleans the room… Her and I gossip and laugh a lot. Reminds me of Nancy. Nancy brought me up."

"You would have to have a nanny?"

"Nancy was our housekeeper."

"That's worse than having a nanny. What the fuck your

brother go do that for?"

"He didn't like people. He takes after my mother, beautiful, talented and self adoring. He'd fly to Milan to buy a suit…"

"Not the suit?"

"My mother bought me that but it'll be Italian for sure. She and Geoff had similar tastes – Dad's bank account."

"Talk about Geoff?"

"No!"

"Have you told anyone?"

"No!"

"Tell me, get it out of your system?" said Jim.

"Why should I?"

" 'cos we get on and you bedded Trev."

"Trev said you were good at games."

"Best if I had been good at lessons. Trev was. You saw his car. Go on, tell me about your brother?"

"On the rugby field Geoff was applauded. He was an ace at cricket but he had this annoying habit of taking stuff. He bought himself some stupid car, costing more than a house. Used one of Dad's credit cards. He took Dad's headed notepaper and typed himself references. People bowed to his affluence."

"How much?"

"Couple of quid."

"Tell me how much?"

"Shut up."

"Tell me."

"A quarter of a million last count."

"Jesus Christ! Your father went ballistic?"

"Dad was not pleased. He stopped Geoff's allowance and informed the police."

"He brought in the cops?"

"Yeah, I thought that. It was well over the top. Told him off. He said Geoff was out of control. Took after his mother. Dad was divorcing her and it had him way off balance. Dad flew to Japan. It was then Geoff punished him, scarred my lovely father's conscience for life. And I guess Geoff punished the train driver too who wouldn't have eaten his dinner that night."

"But your dad would like you best?"

"Of course. He supports no-hope badly run charities. And I am flawed with a capital Fuck. Geoff was good at school, good at games and Oxbridge bound. I loathed games and left school excelling in skiving and was expelled after being thrown out of a pub drunk. The headmaster thanked me for not wearing school uniform. Said he did not want it tainted by an excrescence such as I…"

"You don't drink much."

"I am lusting for those feet again. I've a bottle in my room for nights. Can't sleep. That's why I cycle, never drive, and mornings I take aspirin automatically."

"Go on?" he said.

"You can't be interested?"

"Bloody am. It's fascinating and kind of scary, like there's no hope in the world. I mean hearing about rich folk who have everything I dream about and they fuck up big time."

"Gives you hope, seeing decadent me?"

His face shone evil humour. "You're my role model, Jacob. I want a photograph. I want to be like you, thrown out of a top public school, ride the bike when pissed and live in the hotel and be waited on by doting staff."

"Enough of this shit, I am beach-bound seeking sex. James, the horses! Where is my fucking fucking-carriage?"

"Near the staff side-entrance. Pumped up its tyres – nice and hard, just the way you like it," he said, his cheeky grin showed that he and I were back on track.

At The Colony the sand had dried in the strong westerly and was fast drifting; the sea was lively and green and blue. Frank was with the fat man Smith but broke away and hurried over.

"I want to go to Amsterdam."

"You are speaking to me because I am not in a suit?"

"I was so rude. My friend saw you leave and said the suit was Italian and beautifully cut. And seeing you on the beach I like you so much and am sorry." His dark eyes studied me.

"I have to join my ship beginning of October."

"There's time. We go for a few days only. Not expensive. Give me spending money? We share a double bed." He picked up a blade of coarse seagrass and ran it down my back. We were communicating now money was on the table. He cuddled me. "I like the way you don't act camp." Laughing he flopped his wrist.

"Amsterdam is expensive," I said, remembering Jim's warning.

"Why do I waste time with other men while you are here?" We talked for awhile and then his stealthy fingers crawled between my legs; both his hands were moving and he had me coming in seconds.

I was recruited.

"Jacob, I come shopping with you and choose your clothes for the holiday?" His words muffled as his soft mouth was on my cheek.

My heart was thumping as I suggested lunch the following day.

Desperately looking forward to the day with him yet when he was rudely late commonsense told me I was a fool. Embarrassed that I was hogging a table, I ordered a starter and a bottle of wine then went to the washroom to check out the car park. Through the small window I saw Frank talking to the blubbery Smith who was at the wheel of a Rolls. As they said farewell I scuttled back to my table. When Frank arrived, he bubbled warmth and shook my hand with an intimate, lingering touch that I melted and on a second bottle of wine gave him a gold Omega which had been a duplicated birthday gift to me.

Traipsing from shop to shop, examining and discussing clothes was not my thing but it sure was his. After lunch he enthused about a jacket I bought him from a female shop assistant who had adored him. "This red shirt – real silk will go with your complexion. And the yellow too?" They did go with his complexion but he had the commanding appeal of top models, wear a potato sack or any old thing and he'd look good.

In a department store he decided I should have a pair of pink slacks. They were cheap and hideous.

"They are just you. I'll buy them," he said.

In another shop a male assistant, notable for his balding pate and large waistband, gave Frank an instant moue of sour recognition. Frank rushed me out.

In a just opened boutique of male fashion, assaulted by pop music, Frank gazed adoringly at his reflection as the camp shop assistant, just about male, gazed adoringly at Frank. Frank chose three designer tops and a pair of ugly platform shoes. "Fashion," he said as I raised my eyebrows. I picked up a pair of platform shoes covered with spangles. "Why not these for evening wear?" Frank and the supporting cast shared knowing glances, literally at my expense, as they gleefully raided my wallet.

We drew breath over coffee while Frank inspected the four pairs of boxers I had bought him and he wrinkled his distinguished nose in disgust as he handed them to a waitress to throw away.

After coffee a leather overcoat caught his eye. It was calf length and double breasted and reminded me of the Third Reich. He rolled his brown eyes as he paraded in front of a mirror. He was desperately in love with his reflection.

"I must have it!"

"You look as if you're soliciting for customers," I said, my growing distaste at his profligacy at last surfacing.

That did it. He abandoned the coat. Shopping was now out of the question.

When we were in the street he spotted a kiosk for passport photographs and was drawn in by vanity. One set of prints were examined then a second, the first set thrown away.

"I need money for a taxi? I hate to ask but I spent out on your slacks."

He squeezed my hand, told me to telephone him soon. We needed to make the arrangements for Amsterdam.

He was sensing that he could get no more out of me at that time. The cheque I had given him for spending money stung – not my pocket but my common sense and pride. All the time I knew what he was, what he was like but I wanted him so much.

Next morning a message from my shipping company had Anthony doe-eyed and me sad as he told me I was booked on a flight to New York the following day.

Despite the weather cooling at the fag end of summer I had to make my final pilgrimage to The Colony.

It was a hard slog walking below the high water mark where shallow waves softened and sucked at the sand. The foreshore was deserted. The seagrass was bending in the wind and the sand was pitted with rain. In The Colony the soup-dish mongoose burrows were empty. Not a soul about. Tasting the salt on the back of my hand, I lingered loving the beauty of the place.

Returning on the chain ferry I was not alone. Sheltering on the port side of the car deck out of the sudden pelting rain was a young man with a narrow forehead and one hell of a broad grin. And he had it all right with his seemingly not yet shaved skin and his well cut, thick light-brown hair and the single gold stud in his left ear that glinted a diamond chip; his dungarees were worn open to the navel showing a smooth suntanned chest. He and I met regularly in the late afternoon after he finished work. I would make a point of catching the same ferry and he knew this and looked out for me. Today his dungarees were filthy with grease from his work. His face, spotted with oil, lit up seeing me. Everyday he drank from a can of Pepsi and ate a Mars bar and he always offered me a bite of the half chewed chocolate – it hinted at an intimate friendship. He had no Mars today.

"Where is it?" I said.

"No bloody money for bloody food." That grin at me.

At the hotel, hoping that I would meet him, I had asked

for sandwiches and had put them in my cycle's carrier.

I said, "Won't be seeing you again."

"Why's that?" He took a sandwich for himself and gave me one.

The gates closed and the ferry clanked its way across Poole Harbour's narrow mouth.

I ate my sandwich, oil and all.

"South America," I said.

"Lucky bugger."

"Finish the sandwiches."

"I'll finish these all right." With his mouth full, he said, "You the only one on the beach today nude rain-bathing?"

I wondered if he had guessed that I had come especially to say goodbye and I wanted to tell him but the ferry took only three minutes to reach the Sandbanks side and the gates were already opened and the cars were disembarking noisily down the lowered ramp.

I longed to stay and he lingered ready to natter but I had to rush to meet Frank.

"You got time for a coffee? Buy you one," he said, romantically for the ferry, empty of people and cars, was our own floating bridge. "We can shelter then." The rain was running down his smooth face.

"Thought you had no money?"

"No money for bloody food. Coffee okay. Okay?" That grin again.

"Got to meet someone," I said and then chancing my arm, said, "Came especially to say goodbye. Really going to miss you."

"Next summer, make a date with my Mars." He put his helmet back on, was kicking his scooter into life, laughing, pocketing the rest of the sandwiches. "On my day off, we go to Brownsea Island have that coffee. April and May is best. Cakes too. Not too many people. See you then." He bumped down the ramp; his boots, held out either side of the scooter, were skimming the ramp's surface. When safe on the concrete slipway leading to the road, he lifted an arm in farewell.

Frank arrived late. Cona coffee cooled in thick cups between us on the grey topped table in a cafeteria bleak with Formica and there I broke the news that Amsterdam was a non starter.

He closed his eyes, opened them, looked away. "You don't mind if I don't go out with you tonight? I've been ill all day." He blushed. Perfect white teeth bit his bottom lip. His blushing reddened his golden face. "Still so sick." His eyes were bloodshot – probably a hangover – his nervousness made a small muscle move in his cheek. He rattled on explaining this and that but I hardly listened.

Feet away a pallid-faced woman in a cloche hat, dawdling over a pot of tea and a buttered scone, eavesdropped.

"Don't stare at me like that. People will guess," he whispered.

I had been thinking him to be second rate in the conman stakes. His conceit had interpreted my examining gaze for one of intense desire… but it was desire… and it was intense.

The eavesdropping woman in the cloche hat perceptibly leant forward.

"You're soaking?" he said, wrinkling his nose.

"I cycled."

"In this?" He stared at the legs of my jeans sodden and encrusted in sand.

"It feels good." The rain was bucketing down, cars swishing noisily on the road outside.

Lifted eyebrows signalled his contempt. "I had to walk home last night – no money. A man about forty-five gives me a lift. He was driving an MG the last time he picked me up, this time a Bentley. He put his hand on my knee. I told him to stop the car." Frank's face was aglow telling the tale. "I told him I am not like that."

"You are like that." I was appalled at his lie that he had no money. He cared nothing about me or my feelings. I felt disgust for kidding myself it could be good with him.

"He's not good looking like you but you don't have money."

I had given him an Omega, clothes and a healthy cheque made out to cash. How much did he want? That question was soon answered. He had great expectations.

"If you win on the football pools – say a hundred thousand – then get in touch."

The woman stopped stirring her tea. She glanced sharply at me and sat back in her seat, and like a high court judge delivering her verdict, she shook her head.

Next day, I took an early morning stroll in the hotel grounds to clear my head and take a last look at the view. On returning, my heart was in my mouth as I glimpsed Frank in the hotel foyer. He must have stayed overnight and bedded Smith. How he disgusted me. If I had driven a Rolls not ridden a bike I would have been so honoured. I was seething at Frank's superficiality as I skirted the outside of the building. I cheered up finding Jim on duty in the porter's lodge and asked him if he could get rid of Frank and order me a taxi.

That got Jim saying, "Is that why you're wearing dark glasses?"

"Hangover."

"You want I cover your head with a blanket and rush you into the hotel?"

"Piss off."

"Shall we, darling?" His ironic hand was teasing in mine as he led me to a STAFF ONLY door. Instead of opening the door, he gave me my mail.

"That's how well you get treated here. Personal service. And you love living with us. What other hotel delivers you one of life's beautiful people?"

"I'll never forget Trev."

"And you'll remember me and Jennie being at your beck and call. Give up the sea and stay. Tony's been wailing and singing sea shanties all night."

"And you haven't?"

"Watched the late film." A grinning Jim gave my hand a squeeze before he dropped it as he led me into the foyer where I was screened by potted plants and was safe-pushed into the telephone booth.

"I'm off to wind up Frank, talk about the weather, mention your dad owns a bank… That should fuck up his year and have him sobbing tears of greed," said Jim.

I reversed charges to my father's private number. Was forestalled by his P.A.

"He's up to his eyes, Jacob."

"Samantha, we are about to take off. The engines are revving and the stewardess is showing us how to put on lifejackets… Tell him his loving son wants to talk to him?"

"No can do, my darling. A hostile takeover. Violent yet delicate negotiations – your father is so beautifully calm.

He's civilised and winning and they are screaming and wetting their knickers, banging fists and upping the share price as their greedy saliva runs their chins."

"Asset strippers from South London with red braces and money in their back pockets?"

"Got it in one. Not one facial expression from him until he smiles at them before putting the boot in yet again. Phone him at his hotel after eight – after ten might be safer. Your call will be put straight through. Jacob, he's still very vulnerable. Do jet engines rev?"

"Clever clogs."

"Where are you off to?"

"The States then South America. You'd love it."

"Tempt me?" she said.

"Exotic. Erotic. In a week I shall be dining outdoors with a transsexual in a street which has an interesting lavatory smell and there naked seamen light their farts to the diners applause. I'll pay your fare?"

"Jacob darling, I am terribly tempted but am riveted by the storyline in *Coronation Street*."

"That credit report on Smith? Where is it? Your efficiency rating is plummeting."

"Sent it to you by my own transsexual pigeon."

As she listed Smith's nefarious goings on I sifted through my unopened mail, said, "Got it. Do not shoot the queer pigeon."

"Is a transsexual queer? Are you turning?"

"You'll find that out in South America. Bring matches, I'll be eating baked beans."

After finishing the call I peeped out and the coast was clear. Frank gone. The blubbery Smith was haughtily lording it over Anthony at the desk.

"One is surprised that a hotel with this reputation loses

a Rolls…"

Anthony interrupted. "I have said it will be out front any second, sir."

"You have said and said but it is simply not there. How can you lose a Rolls?"

What a prick, I thought, edging out the telephone booth. Smith was standing at the desk. An elderly couple were watching his bullying display with open distaste as if giving Anthony their dignified support.

Jim interrupted my spying to tell me that he had loaded my baggage into the taxi. His fingers were gentle on my sleeve as he said, "Jacob, the mouth at the counter. It's Jennie he's accused of stealing?"

"How much was it?"

"Four hundred? *Jennie?*"

"You should have said." Jennie was motherly and wore a starched uniform that creaked when she fussed over me.

"She was worried sick about people finding out. On tranquillisers now. I could kill that cunt."

I marched to the desk. Slammed Smith's credit report on the counter in front of him.

"And you are?" said Smith, not recognising me in jeans and sunglasses. When I said nothing, he nervously glanced at the report's green cover which was headed CONFIDENTIAL. Inside on page one he read his real name and several aliases, his address, his date of birth and nationality. Page two had him speechless.

I stared at the fat perspiring man who shifted nervous feet. Maybe he thought I was the fraud squad.

I took the report from him. "It says *This man is a thief and a conman. He is an ex convict. He is an undischarged bankrupt who masquerades as a stockbroker and a financial advisor.*" I now had the full attention of the two disgusted guests and the on-duty manager and Jim and Anthony. I thumbed through the report. "You served eighteen months of a three year sentence. You conned a widow over eighty who died of a stroke during your trial. You took her for thirty grand. Your fellow inmates took you in the shower. They cut you. Badly. The prison hospital sewed you up. Badly. They left your face with scars ridged like furrows in a ploughed field. They do that to show others what scum you are. The plastic surgery doesn't quite disguise them, does it?"

"All a mistake I can assure you. Let me explain in some less public place? I have impeccable references and was only dining in the House of Lords on…"

"You tried to screw money out of this hotel by accusing a decent member of staff of being a thief."

I handed the report to the duty manager, who scanned it, checked the agency's name and the firm of accountants, said, "You want a job here, Jacob?"

Smith, trying to snatch some dignity, mumbled, "There's no need for unpleasantness. My things…?"

"Mr Smith? My office," said the manager.

Smith opened a bulging wallet and gave forty pounds to Anthony. "For the chambermaid."

I took the forty pounds, fed it slowly into a charity box. "She has what you lack – integrity."

"Your bill, sir?" said Anthony.

Smith waved a wallet fat with notes. "I'll pay cash."

The manager said, "Bring it in when it's ready, Tony."

As the duty manager led Smith to his office, the elderly couple came up and the woman put her hand behind Anthony's neck and pulled him towards her. As she kissed his cheek, she said, "You weren't alone, I was about to knee the bastard."

Amid laughter, the couple walked away, and my tears welled as Anthony gripped my hands, said,

"You're my favourite guest of all time. Swallow the anchor and stay?"

"Swallow the anchor? Love it." I bit my lips as I put fifty pounds in an envelope and wrote on the outside *For Jennie with my love* and gave it to Anthony. "Left you my bike. It knows its way to The Colony."

I had to turn away, the tears were starting.

Traipsing after Jim to my waiting taxi, getting back to being hard nosed, I said, "That was more satisfying than sex. Can't remember, did you and I do it?"

Outside in the soft breeze, he said angrily, "Why'd you leave it too late?"

"Jesus, how did I know? I'm real shy with you. You're young, the top of everyone's hit list, for Christ's sakes. And you had your friend on the beach…"

"Mike's a mate. Drives me. Couldn't make the move on you, could I? Why the fuck didn't you say, Jacob?"

"Thought it might terminally embarrass you into turning me down or token doing it? We have so much going on between us but I didn't know what to do. Honest. Wish it was you who had been my brother."

"But Anthony chatting you up, didn't bother you?"

"Anthony's Anthony, that's different and you know it."

"It's the class thing. Anthony is middle class and I scrub the lavatories," said Jim.

"Oh, crap, Jim. Inside now? I'm already damp."

He grinned. "You play with yourself thinking of me?"

"You're good. Think of me midday mid-Atlantic and get unzipped. You are joining me in the Mile High Club."

He was openly laughing. "If we had? Anthony would not be talking to me never ever. He can be very moody and he's very loyal, unlike you. You'd screw anything."

I pushed notes into his top pocket.

"Jesus Christ, you're doing it again."

"Money is the only way I have of showing how much I like you and Anthony. I'd say love but you'd scoff."

"Piss off, Jacob."

"You're scoffing. Have a night out. Invite Trev. If he's honest he'll tell you that you and he should get together."

Jim's lips were a tight line. "Like family – you with us."

Anthony pushed out the main door to join Jim and they stood on the hotel's steps both with triumphant fists thrust in the air as the taxi drove slowly down the long broad drive between lines of white painted rocks.

When Jim and Anthony were out of sight, I blew my nose.

Seeing a dark haired man strolling towards the main gates. I asked the driver to stop.

Frank said, through the open window, "Your father owns a bank? Which one?"

I wanted to giggle, have Dad as the sole owner of Barclays but I said nothing. I always knew that I could buy Frank but Frank had set his price too high so maybe I had some business acumen after all. Shutting the window, I nodded to the driver that he should drive on.

The taxi followed the curve of the drive; formal lawns stretched either side, the flower beds were empty of their summer bedding.

JACOB SEEKS RETRIBUTION IN PAUL MANN'S ACCLAIMED ADVENTURE STORY *NAILING FRANK*

ON THE BENT AND NARROW

ONE

My stars indicate a particularly positive holiday for all Scorpions *as the moon moves on Christmas Eve to link up with Venus. This powerful force will have you changing your outlook.*

To help the powerful force along I had packed four bottles of scotch which will supplement my already ample 'cellar' under the kitchen sink in my house because it is Christmas Eve and the shops will be shut when I arrive in Nailsford.

A change of trains after a delay due to a minor derailment had the InterCity filling with servicemen going on leave – loud and good natured.

As we rattled our way through Wiltshire, seated and snug, I shared a whisky bottle with a dark and compact naval rating who tapped the paperback on my knee. "You read?"

"I am tempted to be facetious."

"Your taste, *A Single Man?*"

"You want we talk about it in the heads?" I said.

"You said heads. You read and you've been at sea? I am thinking Hello Sailor!" He hauled me out of my seat.

As I was locking the lavatory door his hand was moving inside my jeans.

He said, "Sorry, my libido is showing."

"Libido away."

The train was slowing.

"Shit, my station," I said. "You a Scorpio?"

"You can tell from me doing this?" His hand was now moving urgently.

"I've gotta change trains," I said, pushing down my jeans.

"Stay on. Come stay in my flat? Welcome to Shangri-La!"

I leant forward as he used tissues.

"Wow. You should be patented and packaged. Gift wrapped for Christmas."

"We're okay together," he said.

"And how. I feel real selfish leaving you."

"How about Penzance? Just me otherwise I am condemned to my sister-in-law and her ten thousand kids enjoying themselves. Paper hats and getting pissed and jolly smiles from a lonely sailor home from the sea." He opened the door after he had zipped me up.

"Reeking of seaweed and beautifully cynical. Nailsford for lonely me," I said.

"You don't fancy Penzance with a drunken sailor?"

"If only. I've got to pack. Moving house, removal van booked."

As we pushed through the jam of naval ratings in the corridor, he said, "Give you a hand with your luggage?"

"I'll wait on the platform and wave you Good Bye."

"You're an old romantic. You got a boyfriend?" he said.

"Sort of. Not a match made in heaven."

Impulse had us holding hands not wanting to let go. I wanted to embrace him but with an audience of half-cut matelots going on leave that was not on.

On the platform, watching the train disappear, I

checked my watch. Time for a drink.

The woman, serving behind the station buffet bar, had that precise unreal speech of domestic servants in geriatric black and white British films.

"Excuse me, sir, this other gentleman is next. Would you be good enough to wait your turn?"

"Right," I said, knowing darned well that the other man wasn't next but as I was a bit pissed I thought that she might be putting me in my place. When she got around to serving me a Guinness with a whisky chaser she undercharged me as she meticulously counted out my change on the counter. I didn't have the heart to tell her because she was so efficiently inefficient. She looked like Gandhi in a black wig.

A handsome young couple smiled at me sympathetically. With their piled luggage and suntans I guessed they had been on vacation to Lake Titicaca or some obscure corner of the world. Even to queer me, her looks were quite something and he was a sexy hunk who carried his topcoat which was a hearthrug of sheepskin, but I was distracted by a more down to earth man in denim.

"Know if the Nailsford train is on time, mate?" he said, sitting opposite me.

"You've time for one. A lager?"

We settled talking until an announcement by a man speaking into an empty oil drum had me downing my Guinness.

Outside was the racket of a braking train. People hurrying to it. Train doors opening had me giving my new drinking partner my scotch to finish before we left the buffet to share the same compartment, talking all the time.

Several miles before Nailsford the train stopped at a small station in the back of beyond.

He said, "We're getting off here."

"I've had a couple of drinks but sure as hell this ain't Nailsford."

"Have faith." He took hold of my grip and I followed him dog-like onto a station platform which was out of a ghost film. No waiting room, no ticket collector – it was deserted. The countryside about us was ink black, no moon, no farmhouse not one building showing a light. The cold lamps which had illuminated the bleak station platform clicked off. I then hoped there might be sex. He was butch and quite something and I am a sucker for the West Country accent.

A torch shone. A woman's voice. She ran up to welcome Jeff.

"Dad says it's too cold to snow."

I sat in the back of the car as we three talked our way to Nailsford.

"You doing anything for Christmas?" said Jeff.

"With friends." I lied, I would go to earth and keep my head drunkenly down and pretend Christmas wasn't happening.

"Pity. Ruth and her dad welcome all. Their relations and several fishermen, a good crowd. No booze."

"Dad knows you hide a bottle in the kitchen," said Ruth laughing.

Jeff said, "George? You know *The Spouter's Inn*?"

"My local."

"Next Thursday around six-thirty? Be there."

"That's you given your orders," said Ruth, parking outside my house.

I kissed her cheek and shook Jeff's hand. If only it had

been the other way around.

Sonny's face appeared at the window. His hair was longer and he limped – a footballing injury, I was told. Well-knit and chunky yet sensitive features. He must be nearly twenty now.

"Might have to leave the bike out back, it's playing up." He stormed in, carrying a crash helmet and letting in the cold.

"What'd you want?"

"To give you your Christmas present," he said.

"Put it away."

"What's up with you? Caught something?"

"Celibacy."

Sonny gave me his can of beer to open because his nails were cruelly bitten.

"Where's your car?" he said.

"Came by train."

Disappointment showed in his face. "Got me driving licence. Could have driven you while you drank."

"Shit, I hadn't thought."

"That's what I like about you, you don't say, 'Be careful' and 'Don't go fast' and that." He sniffed. "I tell you honestly, George, you are a very scary driver."

I had let him drive my car fast on the abandoned wartime airfield and taught him to drive like a little old lady on Devon's winding roads. He came everyday and would say "When I get my licence I'll come live with you and drive you, do the cooking for you."

"The park cottage still your HQ?" I said.

"Don't do that no more."

"So, I am the only man in your life?" I don't know why

I asked for I rarely believe anything he says.

"You're my last fag in the pack. And I'll keep you company on Christmas Day."

"Tomorrow?"

"Christmas Day is tomorrow," he said.

"Don't bother."

"Not doing anything, might as well."

"No punters on Christmas Day?"

"You've just done that one, George."

"What did you do over the summer, dream about me?" I said.

"Lifeguard, wasn't I?

"Plenty of women?"

"Four."

"Only four?" I was surprised. Sonny is a magnet to women. Handsome as any film star with his intense dark blue black-lashed eyes. His jeans are worn and sexy, the cuffs fraying, which, he would tell me, is fashion. The top he had on was cheap but showed off his shoulders. The trainers expensive but worn.

"It's blokes surfing and grockles on that part of the beach," he said.

The grockles were families and elderly couples from London and the North. Nowadays the beautiful young burn up and throw up in Ibiza.

Sonny went to school in Devon from the age of eight but I think of him as a Londoner; he has that self assurance and much of the attitude lingers.

"You stopping the night?" I said.

"Can't. Haven't told Dad. And I am doing the milking first thing, it being Christmas Day."

He was suddenly shy, fingering a letter.

I said, "Give it here."

"Don't you dare fucking read it! Just what she calls me. George!"

I pushed him away. The round female hand addressed him as 'Dear Buttocks'. It was a well written and tender letter.

He said, "What do you reckon?"

"Why ask me?"

"Because you're the only person I can talk to."

"You talk to your dad," I said.

"Calls them shag bags," said Sonny.

"This girl is serious. Sounds nice."

"She only took her top off."

This was new. Every girl he has had he has screwed and many have been left heavy with child, all on their knees begging him to marry them. I said, "Don't you want your beer?"

"Stout, innit?"

I finished his drink. "Not football again?" I said as this cocky Cockney turned on the television.

When the match finished, the programme was a Starsky and Hutch repeat. When I complained that we never had policemen who looked that good, he said,

"They had this one episode supporting your lot. You see it? Did you fuck. You knows nothing."

"Starsky and Hutch were an item? That is too good to be true."

"No! I am not talking to you. Pissed you are." He glared at the set.

In fact a friend had taped the programme and when I had watched it I had got a tingle in my testicles immersed in that queer life of disco music, dustbins in alleys, extractor fans pushing out air stinking of booze, and men passing through a door into a club with a dance floor, above which rotated a mirrored glitter-ball raided from some long gone palais de danse.

"Saw it, Sonny. And you're right, I was at home. Home is a bar where tobacco darkens the ceiling, where a barman hands out cigarettes, where all the customers are from my clan, where a resplendent old man with pencilled eyebrows and a broad brimmed fedora is not commented on, and where the beautiful young are vain. The young pout, waiting for sex, squandering their youth. That's my home. Sure as hell it ain't yours. But I see you there now and I know we shouldn't be together, but we are. Why, Sonny? Why?"

"Good job I'm used to you talking shit." He wrinkled his nose, happy again.

"You only came to get fifty pence for the disco," I said.

"More of your shit. The disco is shut."

He was probably right for Bogart was on the screen and we were into the late night movie.

"You know that man in the pub last May?" he said.

"No."

"Shuddery in a mac?"

"Yeah, got you. Depressing. Lurked, eyes on you all the time. Made me think of a winter-cold urinal; two men panting and a squalid paragraph on the back page of the local paper," I said.

"That big pouf spent ten quid each on us dinners. I had two lots of corn on the cob. And lagers." He hesitated and I knew that he might be exaggerating but not lying. "He didn't do nothing to me. I lay there."

"Did he ask for a refund?"

Sonny lowered his voice and had stopped biting his nails so I knew he was telling the truth. "It's only you now. Came to see you last night. And the night before.

George, make me cheese sandwiches?"

"Only got margarine. And the cheese is heading for penicillin."

He grimaced, said, "Fuck off." but grinned when I said we'd go out to see if a corn on the cob takeaway was open.

"How much do you want if we have sex, Sonny?"

"Three-pounds forty-five for the bus fare. There's this girl in Tavistock, she wrote the letter."

"Two pounds is your going rate. Is this an extra for the festive season?" I said.

"I am no liar. Read." He handed me a bus time table and where his wet finger pointed I read £3.45 in a blur of small print. "And I didn't ask for no money."

"You don't want money?"

"Things are different. I've stopped doing park-jobs."

I threw four pounds on his lap and told him to piss off. He watched Bogart not nail chewing and told me he would be joining the army on the twenty-first of January, that's why he wants to go to Tavistock to say goodbye to Lila.

"All the months you were away I came round here three times a week to see if you'd come back. Not for no money," he said.

"You've just put it in your pocket."

He took it out and gave it to me, didn't say anything but stood and we were face to face. His face showed hurt. He wanted to stay and talk. He was worried about going in the army. I can make Sonny cry, I can hurt him, screw him up. He was about to rush out the door but I caught his arm, pulled him back into the room.

Sad faced he sat down.

I switched off the television, said, "Tell me?"

"Got called a poof, didn't I? In the pub."

"Tell me?"

"Larry Big Gob. He's twenty-five. I knocked the shit out of him. I got scared."

"Why scared?"

"I leaves the bastard for dead on the pavement, blood running from his mouth and him not moving with the police sirens nearing."

The fight I believed but its details would be wildly exaggerated. Sonny has a boxer's physique but not the sadistic desire to beat anyone to pulp.

"The heater on in the bedroom?" he said.

I followed him upstairs. His skin was smooth and winter white. When I was inside him and my hands were on his sex, there was a connection between us there never had been before and its intensity embarrassed us as we climaxed. So powerful that he let me stay there and I wanted to sleep all night, resting my face warm on his broad back.

As I washed afterwards my hands shook as though I was unwell; knowing it was the feelings I had for him.

He was back in the front room dressed with the TV on and was comfortable with me; controlling me now. He helped himself to a handful of coins off the mantelshelf, having decided to go for cigarettes at two in the morning. "There's a machine in a hotel foyer." He came back sober with cigarettes.

After he settled on his return, I said, "You forgot to take the rest of the loose change."

"I don't do no loose change."

"You just did."

"I'll come tomorrow," he said.

"Today. Merry Christmas." I tucked four pounds in his pocket. "That'll save you coming."

“Let you be by yourself at Christmas? When I offers to come here like a good Christian? You’re crap at relationships. That poor wife of yours? She left you, I bet. I’ll come. Keep you company.”

“It’s finished. Take the loose change out the offertory box on your way out and have a cool Yule.”

Sonny has difficulty taking anything I say seriously. He dealt with the situation: “You can’t spend Christmas alone.”

“Don’t you understand the phrase, Fuck off?” I said.

“When you were upstairs I took a chicken out to defrost for us Christmas dinners, that’ll put you in a good mood for a change.”

“I…”

“I’ll bring King Edwards and stuffing. You’ve got sausages in the freezer,” he said. “What beer you got?”

“Schlitz.”

“What’s that then? Lager? I want lager not stout.”

“It made Milwaukee famous,” I said. “And why are we not having sprouts? I want my sprouts for my Yule meal, you miserable lazy bastard.”

“You’ve got frozen. You’ve got bath salts – saw them. We’ll bath together before us dinner. I’ll bring butter. Do the cooking. And I’ll ask Dad for a bottle of scotch. Your Christmas present from me, tightwad.”

Game, set and match to Sonny.

TWO

My Nailsford house is a solidly built terrace, faced with brick over stone and the stone is a beautiful mix of soft browns and terracotta, the brick is white and shiny and reminiscent of a public urinal. How times change, stone is now in vogue so are public urinals when Sonny isn't around.

The place is all but sold, for contracts have been exchanged, but I haven't the heart to finish packing; packing is so final and Christmas with Sonny was memorable and I don't want to leave.

He rushed in flushed red, not bothering with the bell, told me he was "now cash-in-hand – doing casual." Could he borrow fifty pence? He needed the money because he has stopped doing park-jobs.

I pointed to the mantelpiece. "Anything to keep you on the bent and narrow."

He helped himself, showed me the fifty pence piece.

I was packing my souvenirs: an ebony carving from Beira, a Murano ashtray from Venice… Events, places and people and dates recalled. Memory-joggers. Tears were running.

"You're getting maudlin," said Sonny.

"Maudlin?"

"I know the word 'belittle' too, George."

I blew my nose.

"Say something… You're leaving."

"You'll be all right in the army. Keep your mouth shut at first, suss it out."

He nodded. "You're same to me like my dad is."

I poured the dregs from a bottle of scotch into my glass. "What's your dad like?"

"He's okay him. Dad follows Arsenal 'cos I do."

"Stay but I must finish packing."

"Can't, got deliveries to make and this evening I've got to work."

He might be lying for his social life is hectic. There are

many girls. He has deep conversations with them in the park, in the pub, on street corners.

"I am going to give you your fiver back," he said.

Which fiver, I wondered as I automatically refused. He knew I would. If I had said yes, he would have laughed.

Forgetting he had had fifty pence I put a pound on the table near him.

The pound was scooped up.

"I'll come in two days," he said.

"I'll be gone in two days, Sonny."

He was silent. Nails in mouth. "I'll come in two days. Just fucking said, didn't I?"

His scooter started, then stalled, then fired again and made an irregular popping sound. My neighbour, a man with no hair and the most dreadful porcelain teeth, who doesn't like foreigners or queers – that's me and Sonny top of his hate list – hurried back into his house after Sonny shouted at him, "What you staring at, baldy?"

Sonny may be crude and rude with me but when he is with strangers he is always polite. Sonny was very upset at my leaving.

He made a dramatic noisy u-turn and came skidding back to shout at me.

"Be in the pub at seven. Only got an hour."

In the familiar warm pub with noisy hail outside coating the windows and making them white, I sat opposite Sonny who tapped my pockets for cigarettes which were in my flight bag on the carpet.

He grudgingly gave me one of his. "You never buy any. We can use Pete's room?" He nodded at the barman.

"Shan't see you again. Don't want to remember our last

day with a quick wank."

"You're a loner, George. You're going to miss me."

"The fags? How come you're so flush? The cottage industry booming?"

He lifted a disdainful nose. "You never listen. I've got this job at this rich geezer's place. He's very…" Sonny made kissing gestures while he moved his head effeminately… "I didn't let on that I know another of his lot – you. Kitchen work today. Mary is ace at pastry. Vol au vents and éclairs. They got this big do on New Year's Eve."

He opened the brown paper bag on the table. Inside were two sausage rolls still warm; the pastry was light and flaky. I ate one, it was delicious; said with my mouth full, "You want the other one?"

"I've had six. Mary likes me."

"Oh, Christ, you haven't…?"

"No, she's old. Your age." Sonny was chipper. "After you sell up, you can spend weekends up here, stay at Dad's. You're okay fishing with the lads in winter. If it's blowing a gale we'll have a few ales in here. I've stopped telling the lads you're my uncle." He nodded at the barman. "Pete says you're okay so you're in."

"Come round tomorrow? Please?"

"You don't never listen. Working at this geezer's house all day. This do he's got on."

Pete brought over two lagers and a bowl of crisps.

"Hear you're leaving us, George?"

I paid for the drinks, bought Pete one.

"Sonny's always on about how he drove your Lotus," said Pete and added, "Told him you can use my room."

"You're one in a million, Pete." I examined his face. "You okay?"

"Been fucking crying, haven't I?"

"It's his brother," said Sonny to me, "Go talk to him."

Taking sixty Rothmans out the flight bag, I placed forty on Sonny's knee and walked back to the bar with Pete, opened a pack, gave him a cigarette.

He said, "You know Tony, my elder brother? Dark, wild hair?"

"Sure. Kind of tough looking but gentle and funny."

"In the park lavatory. In a lock up with a bloke. After the pubs shut. Half cut. Jeans at their ankles. The police."

"I'll get you a scotch."

"You're all right, mate," said Pete, tears running.

I lifted the bar flap, walked behind the bar and pushed a peg glass under the optic, put the double whisky in his hand, put the money on the till.

Pete drained the glass. "Last week. Him and the other bloke were arrested for Performing an Indecent Act in Public? Public? They broke open the fucking door, didn't they? Tuesday it was when he told me. Tuesday morning he was walking his flat saying all the time 'I wish I was dead'. Told him not to be so fucking stupid and I'd come back after I'd taken the deliveries at the pub."

"Pete? Tell me?"

"Sonny wouldn't say 'cos Tony fancied him rotten but Sonny would have none of it but they stayed mates."

Pete looked as if he could not continue so I said, "Pete?"

"The deliveries came late. Instead of opening the pub, I ran all the way to his flat 'cos I knew something was up. I went straight to his garage. His motor bike was in bits as per usual and his leathers hanging up. Tony hanging up too. Slow turning on a hook. Still warm. Topped himself over a wank."

"Jesus!" I covered my mouth with my hand, my eyes filling.

"Mum's out of her skull. Keeps on about how she failed her son and it is God's punishment that she dies. Doctors have her in hospital, suicide watch, won't sedate her 'cos she has to come to terms with the loss. Come to what fucking terms, George? Jesus Christ, I am sorry to be like this, George."

Pete was sobbing and sobbing. I was about to serve a middle aged couple when the woman, said, "It is all right, dear. Pete's got to deal with it. Takes time. Tony was a lovely young man. Brought my washing in if it rained, telling me my smalls embarrassed him. Always a joke."

Pete said, "George is Sonny's friend."

She said, "Go make your tea, love."

Back with Sonny, I said, "She took charge?"

"Maggie owns the pub. Pete always ran it but since Tony topped himself she keeps an eye on him. She or her bloke will watch the bar until Pete gets it together."

Sonny and I were silent and Sonny had such misery in his face and his fingers were in his mouth but all nails had gone.

He brightened. "Told Dad I am engaged."

"What did he say?"

"Laughed. I am going to tell him about you," he said.

"Why?"

"Show him I am a serious human being."

I studied him. "Pete's brother's death got to you?"

"The cottage. Can't go there."

"You're not queer but you're taking a stand, why?"

"I'm off soon 'cos I won't be finished work until after midnight then milking first thing." Sonny stood, leant on my shoulders, said, "If I am not queer why do I like you fucking me?"

I tucked an envelope in the pocket of his denim blouse. "You're my therapist. A psychiatrist I would have to pay a fortune to get useless advice. Sonny, tell Pete…"

"No, you tell Pete."

"Me?" I held Sonny's wrist.

"Go talk to him. Like now."

I stood, picked up my flight bag, turned towards the bar.

"And come back for his brother's funeral. Bring the Lotus. That'll show the fuckers."

As Maggie lifted the bar flap to allow me to go through to the back room, she said, "Get Pete to talk about their time growing up. How Tony came home from school with blood on his lip and told him he was queer. Made them close. Pete was fourteen. Looked up to him ever since."

I was almost crying.

She said, "Listen to him?"

"Long as he wants," I said, hearing Sonny leave through the front door. This was the last we would see each other but neither of us could say goodbye.

THREE

Last night I lay in bed listening to the small stream which runs the end of my back garden, sipping scotch, waiting for it to put me to sleep.

It's afternoon and the removal men have been and gone, leaving doors open while they emptied the house making the place unbearably cold. Tonight I should book into a hotel but do not want to break my connection with the house, my last link to Sonny who might come round so

I'll make do with sleeping on an inflatable Lilo in front of the gas fire. This winter is a battle with the endless cold. I am wearing two heavy sweaters, ski pants, zip up leather boots and my teeth are chattering so much that I had to stop writing this to crouch over the gas fire while waiting for water to boil. I made tea and drank it out of a mug stained with red wine. I followed my tea with a mug of instant soup. Warmed, I had to go out for I cannot bear the empty echoing rooms.

A woman could not keep her footing on the icy steep slope of pathway. And in the companionship, which the drama of British extreme weather brings, I grasped her arm as she slid.

"Hold onto me!" I said.

She hesitated.

"I'm queer. You're safe," I said.

She clung to me and when more secure on the flat, arm in arm, we chatted our way across the bridge. Tide out, fresh river mud glistening frost. Small puddles of seawater were already ice. Rounds of ice floated on the still water. Reaching the other side of the river, we climbed a hill to stop outside a line of slate-roofed stone houses.

I said, "Saw you on the railway station before Christmas. Talking to a hunk wearing a sheepskin coat?"

"Pierre. We were met by Torquil."

"Who?"

"Pierre stays with Torquil, and looking the way he does he gets away with being a slob."

"Pierre is queer?"

"You wish. Torquil is. Torquil's house is filled with beautiful objects. Antiques and good paintings – and Pierre. Torquil's latest acquisition is a dial-in-youth who works for him on a casual basis. Looks an angel."

"Another artefact like Pierre?"

"An artefact is a manmade object," she said.

"This angel got a name?"

She shrugged. "Estuary-speak."

Sonny.

"I'm a journalist. Pierre makes money as a model and I have a thing about him. I stay with Mother." She pointed to a small terrace house. "Come in. She's got a Dachshund trained to savage rude men."

"And you're not rude?"

"Torquil is holding a charity do tonight. I'm taking photographs. Come as my acid tongue?" she said.

"To make Pierre jealous? No way."

"I'm not a bitch." An address card was put in my pocket. "Ring before eight. I'm Stephanie. You'll love Pierre."

"I'm George."

"Come in and meet Mummy?"

"For ten minutes? I've an appointment."

"Ten minutes makes you unavailable and irresistible. I am lusting." She laughed, opened the front door and pushed me into a warm livingroom. She cuddled a welcoming dog, at the same time calling, "Mummy, come meet George he needs a cup of tea before he has to race off to an appointment."

My appointment was with a man who bought me a scrumpy. SCRUMPY NOT TO BE SOLD TO VISITORS a notice warns in *The Spouter's Inn's* public bar but we were in the back parlour which the locals use.

There is a brown varnished dado and the wood chairs are pre-War dining-room solid and weekly polished.

Seated in front of a coal fire was Ruth and the sexy man I'd ran into in the train station buffet before Christmas.

Jeff must be immune to the weather for his shirt was open at the neck and showed dark chest hair. Instinct had me telling them that I was sad to leave the town now it is so final as my house is empty of furniture.

"You're welcome to stay at the farm?" said Ruth.

"You're really kind," I said.

"Your dad? He does go on," said Jeff.

"You mean he says grace at meal times?" she said.

"He's best kipping on my bed-settee? George, take Ruth's key and let yourself in. Windy Side, know it?"

I nodded it was Sonny's street.

"You'll be watching soccer," said Ruth laughing.

"Arsenal?" I said.

"A supporter? You'll be at home with my son."

"You're as lifesaver, Jeff," I said. "Excuse me – a telephone call."

"It'll be a girl," he said.

"And a looker?" said Ruth.

"Very rude to me."

"That's love," he said.

"It sure ain't love."

I made my way to the pay phone in the small hall.

The Torquil gathering reminded me of the Welcome on Board cocktail party for First Class passengers in cruise ships so I was wondering how I could make a break for it and look for Sonny.

"Is this too tedious?" asked Torquil in a flat upper-crust voice. "I've arranged for you to eat upstairs away from the masses."

"No to food. I am not going to put you out."

"You won't. Pierre has cooked enough for ten." He looked at the crowd of well-heeled folk talking, laughing and drinking. "You'll love Pierre. Wish I could love this lot." His voice showing disdain. "Got them off a list. Very little between the ears or anywhere else to interest me." His grip on my arm tightened pleasantly.

Silver-haired, lean and elegant, he guided me between groups as we made our way into the vast room illuminated by pools of light from many table lamps. He introduced me to a woman with wild long dark hair who wore a Laura Ashley dress.

"That medical friend of yours? Is he coming, Torquil?"

"Only if he can get the huskies harnessed."

"I am desolated! A physician who graduated in charm and is wonderfully black and criminally sexy."

Torquil guided me away and said in his seductive monotone, "They talk about sex when they should talk about giving to charity."

"Or the weather?" The snow was heavy and settling.

"What do I do with them, George?"

"You'll have tried the hotels?"

"I telephoned those within walking distance. *The Old Soldier* is taking eight. I shall have to bed and breakfast God knows how many. It'll be the Blitz, my dear."

Torquil's face conveyed amused alarm as we eaves-dropped on a young man, with a trace of African blood, say to an equally young friend, "The second court case was what?"

"I was Outraging Common Decency."

"What's that then?"

"A year – suspended sentence."

"But what's Outraging Common Decency?"

"It's like Gross Indecency but more refined. In a shop."

"Not Harrods?" enthused the good looking lad.

"Piss off. One of them kiosks that takes them passport photographs in a supermarket."

An interesting conversation. I was hooked.

The questioner, who had a small ugly star tattooed in blue and red on a sexy broad dark neck, said, "You didn't have the curtain open?"

"Curtain's short, innit?"

"And?"

"And what?"

The guy with the sexy neck said, "You know fucking what."

"I was Outraging Common Decency and this granny barges in. Her screams brought the men in suits. I was frog marched to the office."

"Homo erectus," said the good looking lad.

"You what? She was on about her photo was for her passport. Going to Perth to see her darling son, first time in twenty fucking years. Lying bitch. Perth's in Scotland."

"Did you…?"

"Scrubbed the kiosk floor with disinfectant. All the old slags who worked there were pissing their boots. Turned them on, I reckon."

"You sign the photos?" The sexy guy caught my eye and winked, and we shared an exciting moment of communication.

But Torquil's arm was in mine propelling me out of earshot. "I prison visit. They've gate crashed. Where is Pierre?" He glanced nervously about.

"You want rid of them?" I said. If it was me I'd book them for the evening.

"Might be for the best?"

I approached the two lads. "Let's see your invitations?" Both had expressionless faces and I was wondering how to play it when the guy of mixed race said, "Thought we'd be welcome?"

"Invitations?"

He helped himself to a fresh drink from a passing waitress as if to test me.

I nodded at an imposing tall guest in black near the door. "He's security."

"You sure we're not wanted?" said the dark young man unperturbed.

I lusted after him and he had picked up my signals loud and clear. I said, "Be sensible and leave."

"My name is Othello. My father was an actor or he was the man who worked on our roof." Othello watched Torquil with a wry smile but spoke to me. "He don't recognise me? Do he?"

They downed their drinks. The sexy young man gripped my arm with erotic pressure. And we were communicating as he said softly, "Can I see your credentials?" Othello's mouth was damp in my ear, his tongue flicked once then twice. "Two minutes in the bog and without me touching it, your thighs will be drenched and you'll be begging for Othello Part Two."

He was taking control.

"I am rough trade gone smooth for ten quid. That's all night at your place. Money back guarantee and we'll welcome in the New Year. Just you and me and my big black friend."

He pushed up my left sleeve, stroked my arm, his fingers lingered, caressing my elbow, his palm warm. "Muscles. It's you butch guys who bite the pillow…" His soft palm slow-slithered to my hand, squeezed my fingers as he said, "Penetration when the clock strikes midnight." That hand lingered for moments on my fly before briefly caressing my knee. "Happy New Year, sexy."

Then he was gone, pausing at a side table where he helped himself to cigarettes and slotted them into his empty pack.

Rejoining Torquil, I said, "I am harder than mahogany. Pour water over me and I'll steam."

Our eyes followed the young man as he walked towards the exit where he turned to check I was looking. Then with a lascivious stare he put a caressing hand to his fly and mouthed. "Be my Midnight Fuck?"

Torquil had his arm about my waist. "You could have used my room but he might have taken the family silver."

"He'd have melted it."

"I remember him clearly. The police dropped the charge. He assaulted his mother's boyfriend who was a bullying horror; wore an eye patch – the police found a knife. Othello and I talked over tea and cakes."

"Cakes? He had me icing them."

"I'll make contact in the New Year."

"The January sales? New Year's Eve is ten quid all night."

"Sorry to sound pious, George, but it's hands off for me. A doctor doesn't fondle his patient's private parts nor do I. Does that sound pompous?"

"Bloody right it does. This ain't the Hippocratic oath. It's a business deal. The guy is hotter than cayenne and he's flogging it. That's me talking about a worthwhile business proposition – forget the charity. Pay the money and fuck." I slotted my arm in his. "I mean, Othello? I thought he was pulling my pisser."

"How charming, his vernacular has rubbed off on you."

Torquil steered me towards Stephanie, said to her, "Do not lose him. George has me longing to take him to bed."

His lips brushed my cheek and he left me with lovely Stephanie gripping my hand and I was wondering about the perversity of life as I would much rather be gripping the hand of the young dark skinned man who was dangerous to know.

I was towed deeper into the vast room with walls darker than plum, past groups of people laughing and talking.

"Come upstairs and meet Pierre, cuddly in a cable knit sweater," said Stephanie.

Two spotlights lit a vocalist at a Steinway.

Conversation stopped.

I said, "He is good."

"The man is an impersonator, like an Elvis lookalike. Never works."

The singer's voice was gravel, his interpretation individualistic. Stephanie would be hard to live with, I thought, as I was hustled toward narrow backstairs – story of my life – my body moving in time to the music. And as a bonus, floodlights came on in the grounds showing pristine white lawns and a snow-clad willow on the bank of the black river. Circles of floating ice slowly flowed downstream as the vocalist sang a throaty Dietrich number.

"Shush, I want to…"

Stephanie dragged me across a small landing to a study, to the consolation of Pierre. Big, young and tough looking, smoking a cheroot and wearing a tartan shirt. He embraced Stephanie but she "was busy working" and her tart farewell had him flinching.

He turned to me when I said, "Stephanie said you were

wearing a cable knit sweater?"

"Too warm. Took it off."

"Take off the rest of your clothes and a pound goes to my favourite charity." I put a pound on the table next to Sonny who sat chewing his fingers.

"We were filming the refuges for street children in Calcutta," said Pierre. "Stephanie had to suffer so we swapped the *Great Eastern Hotel* for *charpois* – no room service." Again the grin. "Fell in love with the kids and her." He smiled at Sonny. "You not hungry?"

On the table, set for three, were salads in bowls and chicken breast in a sauce, a cheeseboard and two bottles of hock in an ice bucket. Sonny isn't into salads which he calls "rabbits' food" and was horrified when Pierre moved aside his tomatoes – tomatoes he likes – to position a quivering square of green jelly which had a peach inside. Sonny's mouth dropped open when Pierre spooned chicken breast in a sauce which was brown and cold. Sonny spat out the chicken, shuddering his disgust.

"In the refuge we blessed the food," said Pierre.

"Got garlic in it."

The nail clicking was a frenzy until I took his hand away from his mouth then moved his plate, split four crusty rolls for him, buttered them and put in a cheese and tomato filling.

Pierre and I chatted through our meal. Sonny ate his rolls, said, "Fancy a Coke?" blinked nervously and topped up our wine glasses before leaving the room to return to give me his Coke to open.

I held onto his hand and squeezed, looked into his eyes.

Pierre pushed his empty plate away, said, "You two look right together. Reckon I should try being queer?"

"Doesn't dating Stephanie do that to you?" I said.

"Sonny, come see me before you go and I'll give you your lollipop." Pierre embraced Sonny who swore at him but Pierre kissed his cheek, laughing.

Left alone with Sonny, I said, "You fancy him."

"Wouldn't crawl over him to get to you," he said, his face sullen.

"Go for it. I don't do jealousy."

"Can't with men, can I?"

"You have had your moments."

"With you." He glared at the tablecloth.

"Maybe Pierre sees an innocence in you that I haven't detected."

"Snob you are. You talk like you're superior. You are. Money and your voice makes you that."

"Ditch the sulks, I got something important to tell you."

He wrinkled his nose in disgust and I followed him and we stopped at the top of the stairs watching the people below noisy from drink. I rested my body on his warm back as I explained how I had met his father and Ruth.

As I held out the door key to his house, I said, "Jeff's invited me to stop overnight."

"Didn't know I was going to finish early. I was coming round to see you." Sonny reached behind and rubbed his hand between my legs.

"I can sleep with Torquil."

"You'd bed Torquil when you've got me?" He turned to look at me in amazement.

"I thought you might be 'working' here?"

"You are the nastiest-minded foulest-mouthed bastard ever. I've been hard at it all day; setting up, cleaning and Tom and me did all the washing up." He frowned, his lips tight with concern, face close to mine. "You say anything to Dad?"

"Don't be stupid."

What Sonny had kept secret came out in a rush. His mother had wanted a home for her eight-year-old son so she had married Jeff. And when Sonny was fourteen his mother had upped sticks. "That bitch didn't give a toss… I cried for days when she pissed off. Jeff looks after me. Jeff gives and gives not like you give 'cos you're a mean-minded queer. He don't want nothing from me and he don't slag me off and play the nasty bastard to wind me up." Sonny mimicked me, "*Working?* and *My favourite charity.* And I thought you was my mate."

"You pocketed the pound. Can I have it back?"

"I wanted to crawl under the table you saying that. I hope you is ashamed."

The noise from the drinking crowd was so loud that he put his mouth to my ear. "Wait! Got to phone Pete."

He was back in fifteen minutes with Pierre who drew us into the quiet of a commercial sized kitchen. Sonny perched on a stainless steel worktop, heels swinging; one of my cigarettes in his hand.

"If only Stephanie had Sonny's sunny nature," said Pierre, kissing a scowling Sonny's cheek. He chuckled before disappearing to find presents for us.

Sonny, using a saucer as an ashtray, said, "Pierre calls me a street child – cheeky cunt." His blue eyes shone.

"He does it for me too. Does it for the whole country, I would think. You fancy Stephanie?"

"She's out of everyone's league except yours. You're a snob like her." He said, "Here's Pierre-le-faggot. Bet he'll pat my bottom."

Pierre could not be riled.

"Cost you a fiver, faggot," said Sonny.

"First thing tomorrow?"

"The farm, milking. And the deliveries will take forever."

"The bar closes at one. Stephanie and me are stopping on to clear up, then to her mum's. Three hours sleep, if we're lucky. Back here first thing." The man who was drooled over by thousands who bought top shelf magazines took Sonny's hands in his. "Make time tomorrow? For me?"

"Might, seeing you fancy me. I just might pop in and leave this moody shit at the farm to sour the cow's milk," said Sonny, making a face at me.

FOUR

The moon was a yellow streak in the black river until the snow came then the visibility was down to yards. I stumbled in the road and as the kerb was no longer defined, Sonny navigated by trudging from street lamp to street lamp.

"Trains won't be running." I wound my scarf about his neck. Sonny was freezing, the flakes were sticking to his face, settling on his denim blouse. I slid my arm in his. "Tell me about your dad's girl?"

"Ruth lives at the farm, top of the rise. She'll bring Dad home in the four by four. No way will she stay the night because that means sex and her family are Jesus freaks. Tripping over Bibles. Found one in the cowshed. Pierre said the scotch was for you – too strong for me. Wanker." Sonny lifted his carrier bag to show me; then in the security of the driving snow, he slipped his hand in my pocket, rubbing my thigh. "The army, George?"

"I know." It worried him.

"Hold me," he said.

I put my arm about him.

"You'll sleep with me tonight," he said.

"Jeff said the settee?" I said.

"I'll square it with him."

Never has my homosexuality had such a seal of approval. I experienced intense affection for this sexy whoring youth with the face of an angel.

"Why'd you never have your house done up?" he said.

"It meant workmen in and what with me being away most of the time."

I slipped on the snow but sure-footed Sonny caught me, was still holding me tight when he said, "When I rang Pete I told him you were snowbound and Pete said he wants you to talk with his mum tomorrow evening?"

"Fuck off!" I said, feeling scared, feeling embarrassed, feeling shy.

"You have to."

"Her son who I hardly knew has committed suicide? What do I say?"

"You can do anything with your fancy ways, your expensive clothes, your posh voice. Tell her being queer is natural," he said.

"I've never been natural. Brought up despised by my father. I was an outsider. Still am. Wish I'd been born straight. No one enjoys being part of a vilified minority unless they are a sadist," I said.

"Know what Pete said?"

"You'll tell me."

"Pete said that you said that being queer and alone is being empty. But what you couldn't understand about Tony was that he wasn't alone 'cos he had Pete's love."

"He okay with that?"

"Was he fuck. Pete doesn't do men loving men, does he? He went quiet so I asked Pete why was he grieving so bad? Long silence. Then came his, 'I do love my brother. George got the same shit as Tony. Get George to help Mum? She's so lost it.' "

I started to shake with cold and emotion as we continued trudging up the steep hill in the blizzard; our heads down, our arms linked, closer than we had ever been. Turned right into a narrow sheltered alleyway that ran between two terrace houses where we stomped the snow off our shoes.

Sonny, clad only in denim, was shivering too but to admit being cold was not Sonny, but maybe it was him thinking about Pete that had him steadying one hand with the other to fit the mortise key in the back door lock. Inside he turned up the thermostat while I settled in a comfortable chair with a scotch while he peeled potatoes at the deep white sink, not talking for a change.

"What's up? Worried you've brought a punter home?" I had sank a large scotch, felt better.

"George, get some manners. You're Dad's guest."

"Sorry."

"Know when I used the phone? Asked Torquil and explained it was to Pete. Real strange Torquil was. He pushed through the cocktail party's noisy bastards with his arm about me like he possessed me. Into a small study. Sat me at his desk. Phone in front of me. I felt important. Torquil said I must let him know when the funeral was and must check with Pete if it 'would be appropriate if he attends'."

The back door banged open. Snow swirled in and the regimental line of Christmas cards on the high red-painted mantelshelf moved in the draft and Jeff was stomping his boots on the doormat.

"George, what you done to the weather?" was his way of welcoming me. He nodded at Sonny. "Curly Tops looking after you? Hang my coat over the bath, there's a pal?"

The bathroom was directly off the kitchen and had a snow-coated corrugated Perspex roof and two lines of washing.

When I came back he was pulling off his boots.

"You've had a skinful, Dad?" said Sonny.

"You what? Two hours to drive back. Cars abandoned on the high road. That for me?" He took the glass of whisky I held out. "Ruth's wrist, so I had to drive. Left her at the farm and walked down. I'm milking tomorrow. Both her and her dad's arms are not clever at all."

"Told you this is knackered, didn't I?" Sonny lifted an alarm clock off the mantelshelf.

"I'll drink tea then my bladder is my alarm."

Sonny had chipped the potatoes and was drying them in a tea towel. His father was relaxed, with a cigarette in one hand and a glass in the other, when Sonny came right out and said that he and I were sleeping in the same bed.

Jeff said calmly, "Go on, what you got to tell me now?"

"George is where I spent Christmas."

"Go on?"

"It's not about being with any man but being with George. Told you George and me is something else." Sonny's face was red making his confession. "George has guts. He's going to visit Pete's mum in hospital, talk to her about being queer. You know Pete, straight as a die. Pete thinks the world of him."

I said, "Jeff, I'm so sorry. I'm intruding. I'm leaving."

"George, sit down! We don't do 'I am polite and pissing off' in this house."

I could hear long loud New Year sirens from ships at anchor in the river mouth. Then bangs from fireworks, and rockets were noisy overhead.

Jeff embraced his son.

Sonny's face showed affection as he patted his father's back. "I always come back to you, I swear to God."

Jeff shook my hand.

Sonny said to him, "You marrying Ruth?"

Although shaking his head, Jeff said, "What you reckon?"

"Won't be here, will I?"

"Is that why you're going in the army?"

"No decent jobs in Devon." Sonny was in the fridge, taking out eggs.

Jeff was silent.

"Christmas Day was Ruth thanking God and listening to the Queen. Naff," said Sonny.

" 'cos you didn't come Ruth got upset. It was a proper Christmas with pine needles on the carpet," said Jeff.

"Prayers and no booze," said Sonny.

"Hurry up with the suppers. We've the match to watch."

Sonny tested the heat of the oil by dropping in a chip. "I got Exeter. Remember?"

"On my tod at the farm."

"George can hire a car, drive me to Exeter," said Sonny.

When I said I had to get back to work, Sonny's nails were in his mouth and he was almost pleading when he said, "George?"

"My furniture is in storage. I'll take leave."

"You slipped on the ice and hurt your arm. It's in fashion," said Jeff. "Sonny, get your hair cut before the army."

Looking at himself in the oval mirror above the mantelpiece, Sonny pushed the soft curls off his face. "Sexy."

"If George lived in Nailsford permanently would you still be going in the army?" said Jeff. When Sonny did not reply, he said, "Sonny?"

Sonny gripped tight my hands, blue eyes on mine, tears rolling as he said to me, "Dad's got a heart of gold. If I need anyone to talk to he's always here. I can go see him anytime of the day or night. Treats me like his own. Do anything for me. I see him and I am okay."

As I finished drying the supper dishes I could hear Sonny peeing in the lavatory bowl in the bathroom even with the door shut. When he was in the shower Jeff said, "You married?"

"When I grew up it was not a question of coming out but of being discovered so I married."

Jeff waited for me to go on.

"Sonny and me are good together," I said.

"Sonny said you two have sex. For money?"

"He's met the right girl now. He could marry her."

Jeff said, "You think the army is right for him?"

"What'd his girl say?"

"Load of shag bags."

"Not the girl in Tavistock. Talk to him and meet her."

"Can't keep track. Hundreds of girls but he's never trusted women after his mum did a runner. Not a word. She'd borrowed against the house as a leaving present. Forged my name. Bills run up at the shop. Still paying off the loan, can't afford a car."

"You must hate her?"

"She left me Sonny."

"You never told him?"

"He was hurting bad," said Jeff.

"You've got to tell him. He hates being broke. He looks a dream and queers go for him. That's how he was with me at first," I said. Still is, I thought.

"You come from a good home?"

"I was born into a family where liking people was not normal. I thanked God when my father had a stroke. Prayed for another. My prayer was answered. Nearest I got to taking up religion."

"I thought you was privileged."

"Sonny is privileged."

"You tell him about his mum," he said.

"Me?"

"It's how he looks at you." Jeff's looked miserable. "He'd live with you if you stayed and I married Ruth."

I knelt alongside him on a rag-rug. "Don't let Ruth go. Sonny will marry in a few years."

"You could live here comfortable with us but him and Ruth? Come back weekends?"

"Sonny sees me, and my car signals a different life. He's got his girl in Tavistock. I'll let him be."

I felt the love of the man for his son, and as I knelt close, Jeff put his hands over my fist and gripped it tight. Sonny came out the bathroom but there was no embarrassment nor awkwardness.

I said to Sonny, "We watching the tape?"

"Make the tea. Dad is two sugars."

The two men settled on the settee: one dark with heavy stubble and the other smooth-skinned and fair. When Jeff tapped his son's knee, Sonny got him an ashtray nicked from the *London Hotel*. And when the game got exciting both were roaring with the crowd.

The tea had mashed and I filled three mugs and that had Sonny pointing to a square biscuit tin. Inside was a white-iced Christmas cake. I cut three slices. Bet Ruth had made it.

Steep stairs led up from the comfortable kitchen to a tight landing. As Jeff opened his bedroom door, I said,

"I'll wake you. My wristwatch has an alarm."

I went into Sonny's bedroom which was oblong and narrow, and in the dark I could see his cigarette arcing to the ashtray. I lay alongside him on the single bed as Jeff's voice came through the plasterboard partition wall. "Make it real early?"

"Not much to deliver, New Year's Day."

"You what? There's four big orders for hotels. And the two pubs have full bookings in their restaurants."

After Sonny said good night to his father, he said to me, "You ask Ruth tomorrow why don't she like me?"

Because you're the obstacle to her marrying Jeff, I thought but said, "Am I milking tomorrow?"

"Have a laugh what with Ruth's dad. 'Our labour is for Christ, son.' I do the deliveries in the Transit. He'll let you drive the Land Rover 'cos you're posh."

Sonny and me in bed like this felt good, it was us properly being together.

"Do it, George."

"No, the noise."

Silence then he said, "You can drive me to Tavistock, see Lila. Book her and me into the motel."

"You pay?"

"You will. It's the way we are, George. You rich, me

skint. You can wait for me in that café where they sell Cornish pasties then drive me back."

"My wife has the money and we are separated. You wanted to live with me?" I said.

"So?"

"Because I had a Lotus," I said.

"No, I'll tell you why and what I feel about you."

"No, you won't." I said, "You'll listen to me. Your mother stole money from Jeff. He's still paying off her debts."

"Fucking hell! Why he never said?"

"She was money mad. You're the same. The man who bought you corn on the cob? You cheated him. Lay like a log."

"Can't help it, can I? Fucking wanker."

"You bragged about it. You're a whore who didn't deliver. You stole like your mother stole."

As he lit a cigarette, his face showed white. Rockets fired by revellers exploded overhead. Sonny was quiet, maybe thinking about my tirade, then he said, "He stubbed his fag out in the mashed potato." That was a Sonny joke to ease the tension. Despite my cruel words or maybe because of them, the feeling was strong between us. I pushed my hand into his underpants. No sound from him as his jism laced and pooled on his chest. As I wiped him dry with my hanky he was drifting into sleep.

I stayed awake until my alarm sounded.

He was out of bed; switching on the light and instead of getting dressed he pulled off his underpants and stood, wanting me to look at him.

"Sonny, you've got it. Stop dishing it out. Think AIDS. Last night you achieved dignity."

Naked and starting to shiver with the cold, he came

close to me, his hand on my hard. "She take Dad for much?"

"He's still in debt."

"We'll have sex here. I'll talk it over with Dad." He tugged open a drawer, gave me thick knitted socks. "Dungarees at the farm."

He hovered on the landing but came back into the bedroom after I had poured an inch of scotch into a glass. He took it off me. "You driving sober is scary enough."

The kitchen smelt of toast and coffee. "You've been too well brought up, George." Jeff looked at me without embarrassment. "I don't hear nothing, drop off to sleep soon as my head hits the pillow."

Sonny interrupting, soap on his face, said with the bathroom door open, "He's blushing!"

Jeff laughed.

Sonny, having finished washing, left the bathroom door open for me and the door stayed open while I shaved.

I interrupted the two, shaving cream on my face, Jeff's borrowed razor in my hand. "Torquil owns the leisure complex and they are advertising for trainee managers."

"Me?" said Sonny.

"The leisure complex attracts the young. With your sporting ability and self assurance and looks?"

"You serious?" said Jeff.

"Torquil has seen him work. Likes him. And Sonny writes a good letter. Good with figures. I ran a banqueting suite and I'd take him on if he cleaned up his language and stopped shagging everything that moves."

Sonny opened the back door. The snow lay over a foot deep. He brought in Wellingtons from a box outside.

"Is the army off?" I said.

"Don't know, do I? Whatever, you can drive me and Dad to Exeter. Have a pub lunch."

"When? And who's paying?" said Jeff, pulling on his working boots.

"George just invited you. Don't mention me and him to Ruth?"

"You ashamed?"

"I beat the shit out of that big mouth, didn't I?"

"Larry?" said Jeff.

"It was Larry in the pub saying that Pete's brother flogged his arse. Pete went mental. It took Ginge and Sailor to hold him. I punched Larry, then as he was staggering, I dragged him outside and kicked him in the face – like I was scoring a goal. Scared me."

"Jaw broken in two places. They wired his teeth. Can't eat solids. You know old Silas? Face like leather? Serves front bar of *The Spouter's* weekends? Him was saying Larry was drinking scrumpy through a tube." Jeff took Sonny's cigarette and inhaled. "Silas lodged with Pete's family for years. Saw both boys grow up. Silas was serving Larry pint after pint 'cos Silas said to me that he was praying Larry would vomit then he'd make sure no fucker cut the wires on that cunt's teeth."

Sonny said, "Me tell Ruth about being queer? Ruth has the Bible, and George has perverted me to his evil ways. What George and me has is normal." He slotted bread into the toaster. "George, this is yours, so move it!"

We talked our way up the steep hill, ploughing through virgin snow which had drifted to over six feet. I'd love to live with these two men, communicating all the time. At the farm Jeff headed for the house while Sonny and I, with a barking sheepdog at our ankles, pushed our way through snow to the cowshed.

The hard work and the smell I got used to. Sonny encouraged me as he talked to the cows.

After we finished milking, Jeff came in with bacon rolls and a large flask of coffee and talked earnestly to Sonny. When Jeff left, Sonny said, "Might have to help out on the next farm what with them having sheep. No one's answering the phone. Nathan sent Dad over to find out 'cos it's his pal who is eighty. If I have to help… when you do the deliveries, go see Torquil for me?"

"You're halfway there."

It was good doing manual work, being hungry, eating rolls and drinking coffee, being straightforward with him.

Jeff was in the entrance.

"Seen Giles. In the bottom field. I'm back over helping him for the rest of the day. Torquil rang. Six dozen eggs, four bags of spuds and milk. He's got thirty-six people for a brunch, he calls it. Sonny, you're cooking. Ruth has defrosted forty gammon steaks. George, you're recruited."

"Thirty-six?" said Sonny amazed.

"Some Frenchman is helping. They all cook in France. Torquil said he'll have the three best-looking cooks in Europe."

"But my clobber, Dad?"

"You've decent jeans under your dungarees and I'll borrow shoes off Nathan."

Sonny looked at his father. "Torquil asked for me?"

"Yeah, so I asked about the trainee manager's job. He will talk to you."

"Cooking thirty-six breakfasts is one hell of a job interview," I said.

Jeff said, "I told him I had you stopping and he said, 'You've stolen that magnetic man'." Jeff handed me the Land Rover keys. "I've loaded the milk and eggs for the hotels. Do them after the meal. Sonny, not too crispy with the eggs."

"Bread?"

"Three loaves is all Ruth could spare."

"You put in butter?"

When Jeff hurried to the house, Sonny said, "When we get to Tavistock, it's you and me in a motel. Afterwards I'll talk to Lila in the café."

"You and Lila together. I'll wait in the car."

"You won't be coming back." He searched for the right words to say but was interrupted by Jeff carrying butter and a pair of shoes.

When I was driving through the farm gates, Sonny said, "Reckon Torquil will pay me? Extra for New Year's Day? Twenty?"

"At least. Give him a fiver back for the charity."

"Why? I am a street child. Pierre said I was."

"Sonny?"

"What?"

"Give him a fiver back then I'll give you a tenner."

"He'll give it back to me so I'll have an extra tenner, won't I?" He thought then said, "Can you fry the eggs?"

"Yes, I can fry eggs." I was fuming.

"George, what's up?"

"Bound to be vegetarians. When we get there, run on ahead, check the store for baked beans and tinned tomatoes."

"Then what?" Sonny was nervous, wondering which way I would jump.

"You grill the gammon. Stephanie does coffee. Pierre

on the potato peeler. I blanch the chips."

"Okay."

"You finish off the chips while I fry the eggs."

"Okay."

"You give a fiver of any money Torquil pays you back to him for the street children. It could be the best move you ever make in your life."

He looked aghast.

"Sonny?"

"What?"

"Is there any fucking hope for you?" I said.

"What you on about?" He looked scared.

"You're a greedy grabbing squalid little runt."

"I ain't rent no more, George."

"So?"

"I got to help Dad. You're loaded. It's fuck all to you. And with you I wasn't no whore. It was something else." He looked scared. "I know you will go to the hospital, see Pete's mum?"

"You don't know that."

"George, you stop this?"

"Don't ever get to thinking you can bounce me into something I don't want to do."

"You still stopping at Dad's?"

"After Torquil's, I'm off."

"What do I tell Dad?"

"Tell him to give my duffle bag to a working class lad turning tricks because that is all he will ever do."

"George, I only have sex with you now!"

I hit snow covered ice. We slowly slid sideways to stop in the heaped snow at the curb. I turned off the engine.

"Don't treat me like an idiot," I said.

"It's you who'd shag anything," he said.

"Bollocks!"

Sonny's hand was warm on my wrist. "Nicest bath I ever had was Christmas Day with you when you told me how a sailor gave you a hand-job in the train?"

"Can't remember."

"And you picked up Dad in the station buffet?"

"I bought a fellow traveller a drink."

"Fellow traveller? You fucking fancied him."

"Only when I got to know him."

"And you fancy Pete?"

"A friend of yours…"

"And you did mention a guy of mixed race at Torquil's gave you a hardon?"

"I…"

"And Pierre? And Torquil? You would have had sex with them all. Since Lila I am with you and her, and Lila only kissed me." His blue eyes were on me.

"Let him without sin cast the first stone," I said. "With her top off?"

"Pete's lost it. Couldn't work New Years Eve. You know you can help him."

"You've got at least a hundred quid and you're still on the take." I thrust two fivers in his pocket.

Sonny said, "Talk to Torquil about Tony's funeral? Torquil has a Bentley and he knows important people. Meeting him, Pete's mum will see things differently."

"Anything else?"

"You're not coming back for the funeral, are you?"

"No."

"Be proud and come, George," he said.

"Proud? Piss off! If you were born queer in my generation, you were illegal. There were no other queers in town because the queers were all pretend-heterosexuals.

We queers went through life feeling guilty about what is natural. *Proud?*"

"I've never seen you like this?"

"It is Christmas. Hate Christmas. My father gave me a train set on Christmas Day then took it away because I was girlie. Had my cardigan slung over my shoulders like a sissy. I was ten. Ten years old. And bad mouthed by that drunken cunt. Nightly we waited for him to roll back from the pub to switch off the television so we wouldn't see the end of a programme. The house not properly heated because he drank the money. When I was fourteen I put a coin under the light bulb in his bed-side lamp so when he switched it on he would get dead."

"What happened?" said Sonny.

"Fused the lights."

"What about your mother?"

"I despised her for not leaving him."

"Why didn't she?" He lit my cigarette.

"She hung on in because that is what decent folk did in those days. Divorce was for the Sunday papers in the same way before-marriage sex was for whores and fallen women. You've got it so good with your beautiful father. And you piss on him by being a money grubbing whore."

"Like Mum was?"

"Like your mum was. I escaped poverty by hard work."

"And marrying the boss's daughter?" He kissed my cheek then sat back and looked at me. "The hospital tonight? It is you and Pete. You're a posh straight-looking bloke who is queer. Tony's mum was always on at Tony about not having a girlfriend." Sonny took my hand and folded the two fivers in it.

"What you getting at?"

"Pete's mum deep down knew what he was and it made

him ashamed."

"And I give my blessing to that woman?" I said.

"She's a country woman, ordinary and ignorant and grieving. It wasn't her fault. Same as it wasn't your mum's fault that she stayed with your dad."

My mother was strong minded and hated queers and looking back she saw the queerness in me.

He said, "Pete's mum saw what Tony was but couldn't accept one of her own was queer. Pretending he wasn't queer was the right thing to do. You know the way her generation thought. You must show her understanding."

"Hallelujah! I am listening to a born-again Cottage Christian," I said.

"You at the hospital is for Pete. You won't let Pete down 'cos you fancy him rotten."

"You've said that."

"George, you'll tell her she must help Pete by not talking stupid about killing herself." Sonny was rubbing my hands, his voice almost a whisper. "And you won't be pissing off and shitting on Dad not when he's treated you like family. Why didn't you let me tell you what I think about you?"

I started the engine.

"George?"

"Shut it!"

"George?"

"We got too close."

As his hand rested on my knee, I could feel a tear building in the corner of my eye, it lingered, brimmed then ran down my cheek. As I drove on the slush-surface of the road, he looked at me, said nothing but his warm hand moved to smooth my inner thigh. Between my legs it rested, comforting me. I turned the vehicle, slowing in snow that lay deep on the broad drive. The river to our right was flowing black and furious; ice was churning, building up, breaking free, speeding to the sea.

"Drinking whisky before dawn? You wants to cut that out. I won't be around to look after you." Then he said, "Come live here again? I'll tell Lila how you and me are. She'll understand."

I was about to reply but Sonny had the Land Rover door open and he was doubling to the side entrance of the house carrying Nathan's shoes, shouting to a waiting Pierre to move his fat derrière and carry the spuds in.

Sonny was going places.

EPILOGUE

I read over what I had written all those years ago. And then I put Sonny's name in the search engine of my computer not expecting a result. With the miracle of the internet, thirty years later, up came his and Jeff's name. Same town but the address was a limited company's registered office. Torquil would be long dead. Father and son were two of the directors of the leisure company. A third director was Lila, same surname – Sonny's wife.
Jeff would not have re-married.

George is *THE QUEER BUSINESSMAN* in Paul Mann's novel.

THE OFFICE BOY

ONE

I think of Boyd with his wild, curling dark hair and his deep hazel eyes in a pale face, as black Irish. The initial impression yesterday was that he was a troublemaker who hangs about street corners in a leather jacket. He's too cocksure, too knowledgeable about motorcycles – though he doesn't own one – and he knows all about soccer. And this morning, as the watch-expert, he took his watch apart. During the day-and-a-half that he has sat next to me he has helped himself to pens and stationery from my drawer; it is as if he instinctively knows I do not mind. He has sung, drummed his fingers and sworn several times. The child in him showed when he was told off by Hannah for then his face had no expression, the rebuke appeared not to register. Yet yesterday evening, when I said that I would be glad when I go back to sea where I could get some peace, there was hurt in his eyes and he said, "I'm not that bad, am I?"

Boyd has chosen me to be his friend.

Valerie sits at our table and is disliked. Her first words about Boyd were, "Look at him. He can't walk in those boots. If he had any bum it would wobble."

Hannah peered over the top of her glasses. "He's a boy still. Growing into a man. Why, he's beautiful."

Boyd returned to his seat. He was effervescent. We

were to play a game, he told me. We were to run through the alphabet choosing a dirty word for each letter. I started with A for anus and he followed with B for buttocks. When we reached F he was in silent hysterics. He jumped up, held his stomach and Valerie was seething; hatred showing in her round face. Gobble was acceptable and we negotiated knickers and he was obviously prepared with nipples. But the W was quite a hurdle. He was cracking up. He leant forwards to me so Hannah could not hear and muttered, "Wanking." He was going out of control.

"You're too loud, Boyd, shut it."

He obeyed as does a child in class.

Later when he went to the machine to get coffee, I talked about him with Hannah. We agreed there was a strange purity in him.

As it was his break he read my newspaper. "M.A.S.H. tonight. It's one of my favourite programmes."

"Why?" I said.

"It's liberal." He smiled. He moved his head proudly, his mouth opened so that the back-sloping teeth showed and his eyes were fixed on mine. He knows I like him. He reached out with his hand and rested it on my sleeve.

Hannah, with a mischievous glance, said, "There should be more touching."

Boyd removed his hand.

Hannah said, "If you want to hold hands – do. We all should touch more."

Amelia sitting at a desk near us, said, "Trouble is if we had a touching thing everyone would grope Simon."

"I did not say grope," said Hannah. "In this country people seldom touch. I find the contact soccer players have nowadays healthy."

Amelia, maybe sensing the rapport that Boyd and I

enjoy, said, "Cowboy boots with pinstriped trousers! And flares!" Her nose was wrinkled in disgust as she stared at Boyd who was now sorting filing furiously. Then she paused for effect, "I'll bet on skid marks."

Hannah, over fifty, always smartly dressed, said, "Amelia, please!"

Boyd, the normally bright and lively nineteen-year-old, was relegated to being an object under discussion; he concentrated on his work. I rested my hand on his sleeve. He looked up at me and smiled. And when Amelia was out of the way he was chirpy again.

It was easier to concentrate on my work after Boyd left so I stayed late. It was quiet and there were few in the office. Alan was filing at the pigeon holes. Alan is wholesome. Alan is seventeen and is a living doll but he is distanced by his shyness. He never talks about sex or drink but there is a girlfriend he speaks of when asked.

"You been away, Alan?"

"Had the 'flu."

"You still look a bit flushed."

He was pleased at my concern. He is extraordinarily handsome. He wore red shoes and pants of a different shade of red and a darker red shirt. All this matched, all these clashes of reds were marvellously right. Black, heliotrope, orange or any goddam colour would be just right on this well built six footer. He would be dignified naked, in fact quite beautiful naked, although perhaps one would see the beauty not the sex. He looked at me, as Boyd does, straight in the eyes. Boyd has better eyes.

The next morning Boyd was irritating, insisting on doing the crossword during working hours and was impatient when he could not find the answer to a clue.

"Your nose," I said and gave him a Kleenex and he blew his nose but was still concentrating on what he was telling me. "You live alone. You need company. Seriously, I could be your lodger."

"I've only known you ten minutes."

"It'd work. We'd go our own ways."

"And that would be company?" I said.

Instead of following up this life changing statement, he was boasting to Hannah that he drank at least three pints each lunchtime. As it was almost one o'clock, I zipped up my anorak and said, "Fancy a pint?"

Not hesitating. "Yeah."

The King's Head is drab thirties. There are a handful of locals left over from before the present landlord took charge, and they sit stoically at their table and talk, seemingly oblivious to the camp barman and the *Gay Times* sign and the varied men who drop in and – are out.

"I haven't been in here before," said Boyd.

"It's queer. Bother you?"

He glanced sharply about the room then he picked up his pint of lager with blackcurrant. "Is this place queer?"

"I've just said."

"It is and I am here! 'kinell!" When he saw me looking at the two men seated at a table by the door, he hissed, "Are they?"

"What?"

"Queers?"

"Dunno – they might be homosexuals."

"I said that! That is what I said."

"I'll get you another drink."

He shook his head. "I'll buy you one. You can have a double whisky if you want." He thought, said, "Honest, you can."

"You want to leave, don't you?"

"Tomorrow then?" he said.

"See you outside, I want to buy a magazine."

He was waiting outside, patiently like a well trained dog. I had the feeling he would wait forever.

The crossing-light was showing red.

He said, "I didn't know you were… gay. Not even in that place. I thought that was you kidding, taking me there 'cos I never thought of you as bent 'cos you have a deep voice and that." The crossing beacon bleeped and the green man lit up. Partway across he said, "Christ, Simon! And you bought a gay magazine!" He rolled his head. "Duckie, duckie, duckie… Jeez! 'kinell! I don't believe it!"

We had stopped in the middle of the crossing. A car driver pressed his horn. And Boyd with sweeping two-fingers gestured the man. "Up yours!" He was wild, black-jacketed and jumping. The other side of the road reached, he ran the pavement shouting, "I do not believe it! 'kinell!"

I trekked up to personnel and was told that the ship I am to join has not left New Zealand so I am stuck in the office for a month but that is no hardship now Boyd has arrived.

He and I have been going to the pub together for two weeks. We have a loyalty as well as a liking for each other.

Today we went to the town centre for my groceries. This he enjoyed and he ran the supermarket aisles at speed. On the way back to work, he had a short conversation with a girl. I was fascinated by her rapt attention, by the direct way she extended an invitation to go out – which he charmingly refused.

On the left of the road is a discreet sign at the entrance to the health centre, it reads Urinogenital Clinic. I must have glanced at it because he asked, "What's that mean?"

"VD."

"Do not tell me, Simon. Do not tell me."

"I won't," I said.

He was serious faced. "You must tell me about it? They look up your bum?"

I said, "Why are you so liberal, Boyd?"

"What? What?"

"You don't give a shit if anyone is black or white or queer. You have no prejudices. You don't hate – I mean you don't even hate Valerie."

"I heard Miss Piggy going on about how I look a rough," he said.

How the name Miss Piggy suits Valerie cruelly.

"You reckon you are good looking?" Boyd is dark, his hair curls, his face is small like his body, the eyes wonderful but in his biker's worn leather jacket the impression he gives is one of a troublemaker, a lad who hangs about street corners.

He said, "This one girl told me I was good looking. I didn't know her and she comes up to me at this disco and told me that. It really surprised me."

"Hannah reckons you. She says she can imagine you pink and naked rolling on a rug."

"Will you marry me?"

"God, you're so fucking stupid. If you weren't so stupid, you'd be cruel. And stop doing that."

"What?"

"Gobbing – that's what."

"It's hygienic," he said.

“Why is it hygienic to expectorate in the street, cretin?”

“Do you have a dictionary?”

“Haven’t you got a hanky?” I said.

“If I had a hanky and spat in that that wouldn’t be hygienic, would it?” He added, “We’re late back.”

“So?”

“It’s good coming out with you lunchtimes ’cos no one dares say anything to you when we get back late.”

The passageways of the office building are painted light and dark green; there are scuff marks on the walls. Once out of sight of the manager’s glass-sided room, with the three black telephones, Boyd mouthed, “Graffiti!” and he pretended to scrawl on the walls with his pen.

I said, “What we need is a can of spray paint. A huge FUCK in red.”

We were both outsiders. Together we wanted to rebel, to scream our frustration, to deface and destroy. We collided in the small carpeted foyer which leads into the office. It is like being in a time-lock. Before opening the door to the office, I whispered in his ear. “I am falling in love with you.”

Hannah opened the inner door. Boyd was silencing painful laughs. He hung onto the umbrella rack, rolling backwards and forwards. Hannah wanted to know why he was laughing.

I said to Boyd, “Tell her and you’re dead.”

I escaped to the washroom and shut the window, shut out the traffic noise then rested my forehead on the cool tiles. A joke with Boyd – anything for a laugh. The detergent dispenser had a slimy congealed rubbery lump which I pushed off and pumped hard, lathering my hands. I forced myself to look in the mirror. I hate my reflection, hate combing my hair, hate anything to do with observing me. I jump when I catch sight of myself in a shop window. Hate the strange unsmiling face that glares back. The nose isn't bad but there are creases each side of the mouth. Okay, the mouth is well shaped but when it opens… Close-up the white fillings show in the front teeth and a laugh will reveal extensive dentistry further back. The light from the window thinned my hair and I told myself that I am not bad to look at. I can console myself with the flattery of Boyd and our humour. But I am the joke – a forty-year-old male with no sexual liking for females. The fillings showed again as I snarled at my reflection.

Valerie stares. She stares out the window. She stares at the wall. Today she stared at Boyd. It is in these moments of intense concentration that she dreams of Donald. She has just turned twenty-one but she seems to not like young people much – she loathes Amelia and Boyd – but she does love Donald. Hannah broke Valerie's reverie to ask her if she had finished her work? And I could hear her telling Hannah how Donald fixed her washing machine last night and this evening he is scheduled to paper the lounge ceiling. Donald is a gem. We have been shown the three packs of photographs of her and Donald on honeymoon in Benidorm. Hannah and I had great difficulty not cracking up when told that Donald had said that on no account must she apply for promotion because he didn't want her working too hard.

Valerie said to Hannah, "Did you hear *that* Amelia yesterday? The mouth on her. You know what that particular young lady is like after lunch with umpteen scotches under her belt and a fag hanging out of her mouth. She asked the new man in Accounts if it was true that he lost his sex drive after he reached fifty. He's as timid as a church mouse. Donald said I shouldn't mix with that type of person. Donald said she sounds terribly common."

Valerie stared at Boyd, uncaring that he could hear. "And common? – that Boyd. I told Donald about him, and Donald said I was not to get upset and take no notice. He said Boyd sounded a twat."

Boyd was delighted. He brought down a rule sharply on the knuckles of my hand. I flinched and gasped. "Quite honestly, Simon," he said, "if you can't take that, you are a twat!"

I found this excruciatingly funny.

Valerie stopped talking to stare fixedly at Boyd.

I scribbled on a slip of paper *Does Miss Piggy know that twat is the forbidden name for a vagina?* and showed it to Boyd. We were both shaking with laughter. I pressed my face into my hands. Hannah laughed with her eyes and Boyd leant over and whispered in my ear, "You twat!" I rolled on the desk, tears running down my face.

Affronted, Valerie stalked out the office.

"She can sod off," said Boyd.

Hannah said in her Joyce Grenfell voice, "Boyd, don't say that."

"Sorry, Hannah." He was contrite and we were both loving him until he said, "I'll treat us to some pot tomorrow."

"Pot, dear?" said Hannah.

"Marijuana."

He was on very dangerous ground. Hannah's husband is a magistrate.

"There's this friend of mine who supplies it," explained Boyd.

"How much does he charge?" I said.

"No charge. Grows it in his bath," he said.

Hannah went pink as she grew more alarmed. And I had this magical vision of the very respectable Hannah, in her good tweed coat, being wheeled out by the police as she dragged on a joint. She said, "It is illegal, dear."

"Yes, but it being illegal doesn't make it wrong. I mean his lot…" Boyd's finger jabbed towards me. "…were imprisoned and lobotomised in the fifties."

But Hannah's immediate concern was not about queers in the fifties but about smoking marijuana now.

"Be very very careful. If you are caught you'll lose your job – lose everything."

Boyd was big headed now he was a drug pusher. "Mum warned me. I am very careful where I smoke a joint."

When he left the room to buy Cokes, I said, "Hannah, there's no chance he'll get pot."

"But…?"

She does not understand Boyd – the bragging, the need to impress. "I'll tell him if he does bring it in I'll kill him, that'll give him the opt out."

We have a new head of department, his name is Wilmot. He is gentle, shapeless, middle aged and I know him from my time at sea. When I spotted Wilmot talking to a clerk, I said to Boyd, "He's queer."

Boyd doesn't see it, he didn't even recognise it in me when I spelt it out. He jumped up.

"I'll ask him," he said.

Minutes later he returned.

I said, "I told you. He is, isn't he?"

Boyd was incredulous. "You don't think I would ask

him? I asked about my pay."

"He's not getting away with it. Bloody closet-freak. He's coming out."

I left Boyd with an open mouth.

Wilmot has several kids and is boringly faithful to his wife. I grasped his arm and wheeled him into the time-lock so we could talk and hatch a plan before he followed me back into the office to stand over Boyd to say, "I understand that you have been questioning my sexuality, young man?"

Boyd tried to speak but no sound came out.

"You told Simon that I should come out of the closet?" said Wilmot.

"No!"

"You did," I said. "You said that Wilmot was a closet queen."

Boyd was dumbstruck until Wilmot and I burst out laughing.

On the familiar street to *The King's Head* road-sweepers had heaped autumn leaves in piles at regular intervals in the gutters. Boyd ran from one pile to another shouting, "Yahoo!" as he kicked each pile, destroying it. I waited until we rounded the corner, where it was sheltered from the wind by a short row of terraced villas, then I showed him my appointment advice.

"What's it mean?" he said.

"Got a date when I go back to sea and visit queer bars in foreign ports, get drunk, wake up in jail."

"Have to, don't you!" Then he swore angrily and spat in a walled garden. Boyd was the yob now. He ran with Road Runner speed. He turned, ran back to me and leant over the parapet of the bridge and gobbed.

In the pub he had calmed and fetched our beers. "See that weirdo at the bar?"

There was a nondescript man around forty draped over a gin and tonic.

"He has one of those small voices. 'Hello!' and 'How are you?' He asked me what my name was. I said, 'Can't remember, can I?'," said Boyd.

Boyd only sips his lager. He does not drink much and I think he does not like drink much either for he kills its taste with blackcurrant.

"You changed your mind about going back to sea?" he said.

I shook my head. "I must escape that office."

"Why, when you've got me?"

Next day I was on a course which sea staff have to attend. Personnel relations. Calling everyone by their first name seems to be the in thing and, of course, these days gender and race-respect come into it. Gender and race-respect mean not calling the pot a black nor calling the queer an arse-bandit.

The young lecturer wore freshly laundered jeans, a white shirt but no tie, trendy but smart, almost a uniform.

"One in ten is homosexual," he said in a clear well educated voice, looking at the ten of us seated at tables which formed a sort of quadrangle over which we looked at each other. And look we did, grinning stupidly like children at school when someone says bum or shit. A not bad-looking youth with a smooth skin that hadn't seen a razor too much, said with self-confidence, "That's rubbish."

"I am the one in ten," I said.

The lecturer said, "Simon, I have to admire your courage to face your sexuality and place it before the group. Well done, Simon. Well done, Simon."

If he said Simon again I would bang angry fists on the table.

At break, just before the substantial lunch which everyone gorges – except me – the lecturer nailed me and again congratulated me. He bought me a pint. On pint number two he suggested we go for a drink sometime. Then he said,

"Are you with someone?"

"Yes, we are very close," I said, imagining a lecture from him in bed after sex, and I put the boot in by saying, "Why not tell them after lunch that you amend your one-in-ten to two-in-ten?"

"I am not gay."

"You could pretend to be or you could say…" I made a good job of mimicking his voice: "Do you realise that nine people out of ten are heterosexual?" Then in my own voice I said, "And when the hands shoot up, you could say, 'How brave of you to come out as straight'."

That didn't go down a wow. He rushed away to talk with Eva who has sailed with me and she left him to come over. As she put her arm in mine, I asked her if she could make a sudden announcement and come out as a lesbian just for the day?

She said, "He's massively upset. Come and talk to him? Be nice?"

"Crap-speak," I said.

"He means well," she said, as she dragged me to the trendy lecturer.

"Where've you been? It's been two days," said Boyd next morning.

"On a course."

"Psychiatric?"

"Why psychiatric?"

He whispered, "You are very worried about being..." He stood and rested one arm on his so slim hip, the other arm was limp-wristed and under his chin; his eyes closed as he said, "Ducky, ducky, ducky." Then before I could strangle him he said, "I'm okay with you being a bender. Are you?"

"No, I'm not."

He sat down as Amelia approached.

She stood over him. "Haven't you heard of deodorants?" Her scorn had Boyd shuffling indents furiously. "Did you work emptying bins?"

Hannah peered over her gold rimmed half-glasses. "I am sure very respectable people work as binmen, Amelia."

"Tea, Hannah?"

They went to the restaurant. It was nice, Hannah could tick her off but they got on.

Boyd bounced back and smiled, and as the sloping teeth showed, something of Brunton came to mind, about modernity being obsessed with appearance. In the gap between his ridiculous boots and his wide bottomed trousers showed muscular white leg with a few short black hairs. His mouth stayed open, his eyes were fixed on mine. I grinned and he knew that I was liking him. He put out a grubby hand and touched my hand gently.

And in that moment of deep intimacy, Boyd whispered, "Simon?"

"What?"

"I've got something to tell you."

"Right."

"Are you listening?"

"Oh, for God's sakes, Boyd."

He dramatically looked about for eavesdroppers. All on our table had gone to the restaurant. "This is serious. It's about Spiff." He dropped his voice so I could hardly hear him. "He's here, for Christ's sakes. Over there. The wally with the upper-class haircut." Boyd continued with drama, "When you was on your course Spiff asks me in the bog why I went out with a queer." Then, thinking, he added, "That's you."

It was on impulse that I stood and once on my feet I could not sit down so I had to confront Spiff and caught him as he left the room but waited until we were in the time-lock, the quiet zone, before speaking.

"Spiff?" He waited, saying nothing. Maybe I should have tried for his gift of silence. "You've been slagging me off behind my back?"

"No! No, I haven't."

"You said I'm queer."

Spiff might hate his pretty face. "It's not only me what said it."

"You asked Boyd why he went around with a queer?"

Spiff was dying to escape and he moved uneasily as if debating if he could make a break for it, but this he could not do because I had fixed him in the carpeted time-lock.

"I am homosexual," I said, as a porter entered pushing a trolley piled high with wobbling files. The man hesitated before opening the other door, one eye on me and the other on the files. I waited for him to leave.

There was now colour in Spiff's face. "You said things

– spoke about me to Rodney."

"That's crap. Rodney is the gutter press. Might read it if forced to but never contribute." Spiff's eyes were not notable at all; an immediate impression was his overall delicacy. I could not dislike him for he looked so cowed, but I was the bully. "Rodney said you made him feel young again. He was graphic on detail."

Spiff was speechless.

"I haven't gossiped to Boyd about how you had oral sex with Rodney. Boyd and I don't have sex but he wouldn't deny it to you because you have no right to ask. Think about that, cocksucker," I said, leaving Spiff reeling in the time-lock.

After work Boyd and I walked to the bus stop. There was someone noisily bustling after us. Rodney, out of breath, his cigarette trembling in nicotine fingers as he said to Boyd, "Where'd you work?" He knew where Boyd worked. He has ogled him at least a half-dozen times with those lusting, camera-recording eyes. Spiff had blabbed. Boyd shrugged his reply. His was a gesture of insolence but Rodney hung on in. "I asked you, Where do you work?"

I said to Rodney, "Go away."

"They're taking in roughs now, are they?"

As Rodney turned to make his grand exit of the final word, Boyd made a prolonged farting noise with his mouth and he and I laughed loudly as Rodney stalked off.

TWO

When it was nearing lunchtime, Boyd said to Hannah, looking at me, "His lot have got this song *Glad to be Gay.*

It's Tom Robinson."

"That's nice, dear."

"No, it isn't. Simon's not glad to be gay because he likes me and… I'm not gay but I still love him."

That was a moment when I was so moved I was lost for words. Boyd said to me, "I'll come out with you and Amelia for a drink lunchtime."

"Who says we want you?" I said deeply upset by his open declaration.

All expression went from his small white face. He hissed at me, "I'll never speak to you ever again."

Hannah said, "Simon, talk to the poor soul." She stood, leaving us together.

Alone I apologised.

He said, "You really hurt me, you know."

I nodded, tears in my eyes.

As we walked to the pub he had his hand on my shoulder and Amelia raised her eyes to the skies.

"Simon, Simon, Simon. Simon is mine," he said, knowing it would infuriate her.

No two people, unless they are married or lovers, should experience our moods.

On the Monday his face was an ashen mask. He complained of a pain in his chest and pulled down the corner of his eye for me to examine. What I was looking for I had no idea but I told him to visit the sick bay.

I heard him say to the supervisor, "It's all right. Simon will show me where it is."

Half an hour later the phone rang and the nurse said that his mother would be collecting him.

As I picked up his jacket to take to him, Amelia said,

"He'll pull you into bed."

When I said, "I live in hope." I was treated to a despairing sigh.

In the long cool green and white room with the bright curtains moving slightly in the breeze, Boyd was dozing but jerked awake, smiling when seeing me.

I said, "You'd like a big blond to cuddle you in bed?"

"I'd rather have you. I'll come and lodge with you. Twenty pounds a week."

I was going back to sea. The idea of Boyd let loose in my house while I was away? I said, "I don't cook."

"I can cook. I won a prize – a cherry cake."

I tried to stop laughing. He was serious and he looked wan and unwell.

"I could have my girlfriend over, you'll like her," he said.

"I'd like that."

"Yes, you will like her." He said, "You want to give me a thousand pounds to buy my bike and I'll pay you back in a month? I'll do anything for a bike."

Beyond the closed door I could hear two female voices. It would be his mother talking to the nurse. I got ready to make my escape through the exit at the far end, hating the idea of meeting her, knowing she would be my age and I might be identified by her as a predatory queer who was to spirit her son away from his cherry cake home to sodomy with the throb of a powerful motorbike.

As I hurried out, he said, "You honestly don't prefer women?"

When Boyd returned to work a week later, he declared that he had had "the pleurisy."

"My husband almost died of that," said Hannah very concerned.

"Just a touch of the pleurisy," said Boyd.

I told him to stop bullshitting.

" 'kinell."

Hannah was shocked at my vehemence but said to Boyd, "What's 'kinell, dear?"

"Fucking hell, Hannah. Can't say that, can I?"

He was forlorn and she was trying to stop laughing.

Boyd whispered to me, "Why did you snap at me for saying I've been ill?"

I apologised and confessed to a bad mood because of a disastrous date.

He said, "He was only interested in you because of your money."

"I know and it hurts."

"I'm not friendly with you for that reason," he said.

I nodded pleased then remembered about the thousand pounds he wanted for his bike.

Amelia interrupted my thoughts with a loud "Darling, Valerie, still on the pill, are we? Or has Donald had the op?" She rattled her collection tin. I slotted coins in. Then she ignored Valerie as she talked about her to me, "Simon darling can you ask Miss Piggy if she will donate?"

Valerie glared at her as she put in a coin not letting Amelia see how much it was.

Amelia smiled at her, said, "Simon is right. Your teeth are like Princess Anne's." Amelia turned to Boyd, "No point in asking you."

"I do a lot for charities," he said.

Amelia, about his age, dark-haired and pretty, held the collection box under his nose.

"I gave a pound to another charity yesterday and am

short of funds," he said.

Amelia would not let him get away with that. She said, "You can swim with the office team to raise money for the disabled."

"I can only swim for the mentally handicapped. I wouldn't swim for the ordinary disabled," he said.

Miss Piggy, Hannah, Amelia and I stared at him.

He sniffed back his cold. "I don't mind getting the pleurisy for them… It's the same reason I joined the cadets for voluntary service to the community and to help the disadvantaged people in my country."

Hannah looked at me, both of us remembering before Christmas when he was asked to carry shopping for the elderly, he had said, "Not for those old bags."

The sweet youth with pale face, spots and solemn hazel eyes, sniffed again. "At the home for the mentally handicapped there is this kid and he runs about my feet like a dog. He loves me. That tears me up… really, really tears at my insides."

Then he almost spoilt it by adding, "I don't mind getting the pleurisy for them. I am not too bad really? Am I?"

Boyd's poignant performance was knocked into touch by Miss Piggy's outburst: "I am pregnant."

Collective jaws dropped as we turned to stare at Valerie.

Hannah rallied round. "Wonderful news! You must both be delighted. When is baby due? Tell me over a coffee?" Arm linked in Valerie's they headed for the restaurant.

"I'll send it a sympathy card. It'll be born with a full set of gnashers clamped on her fat udders," said Amelia. Before she marched off she turned to Boyd. "You're on the list for swimming. You'll need sponsors."

I said, "Don't worry, I'll get the barman in the pub to put a notice on the board. Good crowd – they'll come in drag."

Boyd said, "My mum will be there."

"Does that matter?"

"No, she's liberal." He thought, said, "Will they really be in frocks?"

Saturday we met at the railway station. He wore a worn-out, grown-out-of anorak in bright orange. He could relax now after seeing me so he ran, jumped in the air his heels touching like a ballet dancer. When he gave me a 'roller' – a narrow beedi-like cigarette – he said, "A Roller is the modern Rocker. Rockers were into Rock'n'Roll, we're into Heavy Metal."

I smoked the strong rollup listening to him.

"Mods ride scooters. We're bike men." We walked by a derelict building. "Where's the cat? It's been three days. Haven't seen the cat to say good morning to."

We stopped walking and he examined me. "You've got grey hair."

"It is creeping down my body. I am greying in layers," I said.

"There's a man in our local who's like a gorilla."

"I am not like a gorilla."

"He has his shirt open all the time, showing it off like it's something only real men have, and you're queer. Open your shirt!" I shook my head. "Christ, you're shy. Show us your leg then?" I pulled up my trouser leg and he rocked, silently laughing at me.

Beneath trees, with hanging icicles on bare winter

branches, stood the creosote-preserved corrugated-iron-roofed church hall. A green padlocked door barred the way. Boyd hadn't a key.

"Why isn't Kenny here? He knows I've got a game. Fuck! Fuck! Fuck!"

I was conscious of the church behind us and how offensive he sounded. When his light switches off and Boyd is angry or in a bad mood he is a plain kid in shabby clothes. Now he was nearing downright ugly until my garden shed key opened the padlock.

Inside he fed coins into a gas meter while I stamped my feet in front of the meagre gas fire and took sips from my half bottle of whisky. Boyd threw me his anorak to hang up and a black leather wallet fell open on the dirty linoleum. There was a five pound note in it.

"I thought you said you were broke?" I said.

He was startled. "You lent it me this morning."

"Oh yeah, right."

He shook his head. "God, I love you." He talked while he set up the billiards table. "Guess who I met on the train last night?"

"Dunno."

"Guess!"

"How the hell would I know?"

"Him in the pub, Simon?"

"The man who asked your name?"

"That voice? Take the pink – in here… You've pocketed it, I'll write to *The Times*." Then he mimicked the man on the train, " 'Hello! Where's your friend?' Then he spots my cadet's uniform under my coat 'cos I'd been to drill. 'You're a soldier! You're in the army!' 'kinell! I nearly died what with the carriage being full and that. Then he says in that voice, 'We gays are human beings'."

"You'd cope." I rested my cue on the baize-covered tabletop.

"The people in the carriage were staring out the window but watching me at the same time in the reflection in the glass. Then he tells me – without drawing breath – he's got this house with a tennis court near the canal, and 'kinell! wait for it! He tells me, with all those people in the carriage hanging onto every single word, he's looking for someone to share it with."

"Why not? You suggested staying at my place," I said.

"But he's queer!" said Boyd.

I hadn't played billiards for twenty years and it showed. Boyd was a good player and consoled me, was patient and encouraging.

"You'll make a good player. Takes practise," he said, chalking his cue.

"Boyd, if you don't want whisky there's beers."

"Go on then. Only the one. I would really like to get P-I-S-S-E-D," he spelt the word, "can't, because I've got this match with Taff."

Taff arrived. Taff was a lanky lad, tense and nervous and alone. Boyd was ruthless and played to win and he pulled further and further ahead so much so I found myself hoping that Taff would narrow the gap. Boyd was superb. He moved about the table with a casual grace and stopped to chat to me now and then, holding onto my wrist as he often does. I was his lucky mascot. It was as though he could not lose while I was there. When the match finished he followed me outside. The tarmac path was no longer black; it was powdered with snow.

"Thanks for coming and supporting me."

It was the first time he'd thanked me, well, sincerely thanked me, that is.

On arrival at work on the Monday, Boyd was enigmatic. "I am not living at home and got a lift in."

I was hurt because he didn't elaborate. Perhaps he was winding me up, trying for a reaction. Then he stared at my Jaeger sweater acclaimed by all. "Hate that jumper."

"You're rude," I said.

Later he said, "Do you mind if I don't go out lunchtime with you?"

"Please yourself."

"I asked very politely and you are rude," he said.

After lunch Boyd did not show up. At three o'clock the supervisor asked where he was. I shrugged.

"He must be ill. I expect he'll be worried about his interview for promotion," said the supervisor in fantasy-land.

When the supervisor rang his home then the hospital, Hannah and I began worrying.

I left work early to search the places where he might be.

On the promenade one of my people was loitering. The nails on his fingers were long and clear varnished, his hair was fine and bottle blond, two earrings in one ear; mascara. We sheltered at the back of the line of beach huts, and high behind us was a bleak concrete wall and I could see between two huts the grey sea break and roll winter-cold on the shore as our hands moved. He rested his face on my jacket afterwards and said, thank you.

I automatically responded but was wondering what had happened to Boyd.

Next day when I got into work, he was at his desk writing a letter. He kept glancing at me.

I said, "You want help?"

He gave me his note addressed to Personnel.

Dear Sirs, I apologise for being absent from work yesterday afternoon. The cause was at lunchtime I went into town and somehow I got into a fight. I hit my left fist against a wall. I went home to a doctor.

Yours sincerely

"You can't put that," I said.

"That's what happened." He showed me his left hand which had the most enormous bandage on it.

I wrote a note for him saying that he had trapped his hand in a door during his lunch break. He had tried phoning the office but could not get through from a faulty call box which took all his change.

"Did you honestly go see a doctor?" I said.

"Yes."

I was silent then he gave me an envelope. On it was written *How can I change your attitude? You were anti me all yesterday morning. Why?*

"You treat me as if I am a fool and now you insult me by lying."

He hung his head, chanting, "Simon, Simon, Simon?"

"You must despise me."

He shook his head. The long hair had been washed, it needed combing. "I respect you. Can I come out at lunchtime with you?"

I did all his work for him because of his 'bad' hand.

Hannah being unusually inquisitive, asked him what really had happened.

I said to her when he left the room, "Let him be."

The next day he gave me two bars of expensive

chocolate with a Cointreau filling. The injured hand was out of wraps and I examined it. Not a mark. He watched me as I dropped his hand then hit it with a ruler – hard, then hit it again even harder.

Unperturbed, he said out loud, “Hannah, I’m off for gay weekend.”

“Yes, dear?”

“Doing his bathroom. Tiling. Show him how.”

His hands are almost hairless and very white and one rested warm on my wrist. Wilmot came over to ask about my tiles and was grinning broadly. But Boyd coped as he chanted, “Wilmot is straight, Wilmot is straight and I am off for a gay weekend.”

“Tiles crack easily,” said Wilmot to Hannah.

Not with Boyd they would not. I could never make that move on him, it might spoil the feelings we have for each other.

Got caught in a thunderstorm, was half drenched. Ran upstairs to the hairdressers. The unread magazines, the expensive green wallpaper, the dark wood and the young man who cut my hair was, I thought, the man who used to work at the rival hairdressers in the High Street. He certainly talked the same way but if I put his London accent on the page it would be painful to read but it is great to listen to. Another reason why I thought he was the same man is the clothes – they are dreadful. His pants are made from a thin black material, fitted at the waist and extremely full about the hips, tight at the ankles in what I can only hope is a fast-passing fashion. It was his hair that threw me. It is bleached now, while back in the summer it was dark brown.

"You're sopping!" His hand pushed under my bottom. Fingers wiggled. "You've wet the seat."

We both laughed as I squirmed and said,"You haven't lost your touch."

"Didn't think you had recognised me, Simon." He dropped his voice, took his hand away, glanced at the girl at the till. "She's jealous. You still a sailor?"

"Yeah."

"You got any pull?" He laughed. "I mean get me a job on a passenger ship?"

"I can give you a contact name and number, write a note saying you're a good stylist."

I was facing the ceiling with its papered-over cracked plaster and the nape of my neck was on the rest of the basin. He was using a hand shower, slow and warm.

"You going out? Tonight?" he said.

"Hadn't thought."

"I've left home. Rows with my brother like you wouldn't believe," he said and added intriguingly, "I took the chance when it came."

If I had his lack of inhibitions I would be a happy man. I grinned at the papered ceiling as he said, "I'm twenty-two, got my own place… I am not restricted."

I wanted to tell him that I loved his moustache for it was bleached and matched his hair exactly. He was round the front now waiting for me to move to a chair where we could talk to each other in the mirror as he shaped my hair. When he finished, he switched off his hairdryer and I was being looked after by the woman who takes the money and had earlier made me a bitter coffee. She represents encroaching heterosexuality as she brushed my jacket.

My hairdresser abandoned his customer and was alongside me.

He said to the woman, “He’s going to see me in that new club near the station at ten tonight.” His hand smoothed its way about my chin. “Should have given you a shave, shouldn’t I?” Then lisping, “Do it later. Won’t cost you nothing then.”

Monday lunchtime I’d arranged to meet Boyd in *The King’s Head* because tonight I catch a train to Newcastle.

Boyd was dramatic. “God, Simon, I’m a marked man now you’ve gone. They’ve moved me into an office with that Spiff wanker.”

“You’ll miss Hannah.”

“Miss you.” He flirted. Looked evil. Dressed in body-hugging black, he is the bad man in the Western movie, lithe, muscular, aggressive and sexy. “Now you’ve gone the manager is on about my time-keeping.”

“Be on time then.”

“Why you had to go and leave, I don’t know.” He paused, waved to the barman now seen as a friend. “Hannah was real upset, us both leaving. She’s stuck with Miss Piggy who sits dreaming of darling Donald and the piglet.”

A man nodded at Boyd.

“You know him?” I asked.

“It’s him!” hissed Boyd. “And he can see I am buying you a drink. Him on the train with the little voice. Him is ‘We gays are human beings’.”

“You’ve made a catch there. …if he’s got a tennis court?”

“ ’kinell!” He cleared his throat noisily.

“Where’d you get that?” I pointed to a small cut on his face.

"A fight. I gets picked on now and then 'cos I used to box a bit. Honest. What'd you do over the weekend?" The palm of his hand nervously rubbed the smooth edge of the bar counter.

I pointed to his hand. "Met someone and we did that."

"What?" He looked at his hand rhythmically rubbing. "Oh, Christ!"

"You're shocked?"

"I didn't expect that, not you saying that." He grinned. "Where'd you go?"

"A club…" I told him of the two women in the men's lavatory and how one squirted me with perfume. "It is Estée Lauder," she had protested when I objected.

"Tell me more, Simon? I am so innocent."

"A beautiful young man danced by himself. He alone was was worth the entrance fee…" As I talked, I studied Boyd afresh, his chin could be stronger and he hadn't shaved, the moustache was sparse, there were some acne spots, his hair needed attention, his shirt open at the neck showed smooth white skin. As he listened, he stared at me with those eyes and he and I touched hands. I felt for him as I have never felt for anyone.

"You ordered these sandwiches, sexy?" the barman said to Boyd, "You are the toasted cheese, darling – tasty and with sauce."

When the barman left Boyd hugged himself. "Listen to him. You hear him, Simon?" Boyd's face was alive. "Where is this club? I am so innocent. Where?"

"Near the station in a basement. Brimming dustbins. Discarded fish and chip wrappers stuck to my shoes as I went down concrete steps. There was a bell and a peep-hole and a bouncer who was black and as big as a tank. A disco where men danced with men and women danced with women and the beautiful young male dancer who danced by himself was the queer husband of the woman who wept her despair as she danced with me."

" 'kinell!"

"Bad in the office without me, is it?"

He smiled evilly. "I miss you."

"How'd you mean?"

"You know," he said. "You're a good laugh. This is our last drink together. Let's get P-I-S-S-E-D."

His hands were making swirls in the spilt beer on the bar counter. The wind banged open the door but its retaining spring pulled it shut again. The man alone at a nearby table was watching Boyd, jealously thinking that Boyd and I were together. Boyd put his warm hand on my cheek.

"Dunno why you had to go back to sea."

It is the delight of Boyd that he would never understand why I could not stay in the office where I had become a player, a topic for the gossips. At sea, amongst the 'officer' class, my sexuality was not openly acknowledged but it was given silent and benign approval. During one long sea voyage I got close to an engineer and he and I pretended not to like each other much but at night we shared the same bunk; that gave the other eighteen officers the sense that our community was exclusively heterosexual.

"He was right, it is one in ten," I said.

"You okay?" said Boyd puzzled.

"You want I write you?"

"You could drop me a card if you think about it. Native women with big…" His voice faltered, he was trying for a stiff upper lip and I told him so and he said, "It's always sex with you."

"It's more than that with us," I said.

"The man you did that with?" He whispered in my ear, "Wanked?"

"Yes?"

"That's all you did?" he said.

"That's all," I said.

"That's you being faithful to me?"

"I imagined it was you when I did it," I said.

"You crying?" he said, stroking my face.

"I would have loved to have done that to you, Boyd."

"I find that really nice you saying that. Really really nice." He was smiling.

The man who had tried to pick up Boyd on the train glared at me with hatred, his smouldering jealousy overt.

JUMP!

PART ONE – THE OFFICE

RALPH

Fifty-five-year-old Alice is into my lambswool jumper. She rushes up to fondle it with me inside feeling not comfortable at all as she tells anyone near how she could not allow herself to pass by without touching it.

"Virgin wool," she hissed. "God! He's wearing it today."

Today is her birthday.

"Would Ralph like a piece of cake?" She turned to Enid. "That shirt he had on yesterday." Her dark eyes narrowed and her lipstick painted lips pouted as she sucked in air. "I could see his singlet through it." Her hands rubbed my back and my shoulders. Her conversation was solely with Enid.

I said, "You are making me uncomfortable."

She stalked off playing the vamp.

If I carried on the way she does, I would be reported for sexual harassment.

Alice has asked Budd what I did evenings.

Budd told her I played with myself.

The large office is oddly intimate. The female clerks want

to know everything. The gossip has me tuning out. And the dramas… A drama is when someone opens a window then there are hastily pulled-on cardigans and moans about draughts. Hot flashes abound. And the supervisors…

At the top table a black Bakelite phone rang. One middle-aged supervisor looked at the other middle-aged supervisor and mouthed, "You take it."

Both men have a sago-greyness about them: the grey suits, the low cost black shoes and they are pale faced and bowed down, dowdily keen, taking their boring jobs seriously. Perhaps they are suffering from despair? I certainly am. I am in the land of the mentally dead.

Five weeks three days. Five weeks four days, I'll say to myself tomorrow, wondering how I stand the place.

On this table of six clerks is a Mediterranean student who is yawning, running a hand over black stubble. Dark skinned Salvatore has the sensuous fingers some Latins have. Maybe his devastating looks give him extreme confidence. I am ten years older than he, but his easy friendliness I envy.

He came over, rested his elbows on my shoulders, said, "Get me a tea, I'll see you in the restaurant."

Then after the tea break he came again to talk to me.

"Why did you say that?"

"What?"

"Why did you accuse me of using rhetoric to impress? My girlfriend said that to me. Two people saying it. I must be shallow?"

"You're only bringing it up so I will say that you are not shallow. With your looks you can get away with saying anything to me. I am queer," I said.

"You don't have to excuse being queer. I don't go around saying I am straight."

"Jesus, that is so different. I was hitting on you. Giving you a hazard warning," I said.

He shrugged his disinterest, then I was put under the interrogation lamp. "Why are you working here?"

"Wanted an undemanding job so I could write but time here drags as if in prison," I said.

"You've been in prison?"

I said, "Vladivostok. Sort of detained but politely while they phoned Moscow. I was given vodka and a good meal. The black bread was not fresh."

"I reckon you're telling me to mind my own business."

The weather never lets me down this winter. Today is grey fog. The bus doors had frozen open, an alarm on the driver's dash bleeped continuously as the wipers laboured on an icy windscreen. I climbed to the upper deck where unseen fields were beyond plate glass windows coated in mud and ice, and the windows were noisily scraped by bare branches overhanging the edge of the narrow road. But I had escaped work. I had taken a half days leave and was heading for my house where Tomas was fixing the central heating.

When Tomas took a break we were both cosy on the settee under a tartan blanket, holding mugs of too hot soup; an electric heater whirring.

I said, "These rolls are warm. Have you been baking too?"

"Corner shop," he said. "I met Salvatore."

"You did what? You mean you sought him out?" I said.

"Sought him out?" said Tomas.

"Sought him out, you jealous bastard."

"Only curious. You going on about him. I read in the local rag that he was speaking at a meeting about the redistribution of world wealth last Saturday so I went. He had on this tartan work-shirt part-pulled out of jeans and hadn't shaved and he looked amazing. Nice body, that dark skin and his hair? Jesus, he should be outlawed. I talked with him for an hour over cups of stewed tea. He concentrated intently on what I was saying while I lusted."

"That's him being Italian. Warmth. That hair? He is something else," I said.

"So you prefer his hair to mine? You prefer him to me, that's obvious. Are you settling for second best?"

"Jesus God!"

"How dare he look like that. He makes me look plain."

"You're a lovely looking bloke and you're jealous of thirty-year-old me with a teenager who is straight? Sex will not happen."

"That cooker in your kitchen? I made your soup on that cooker and you're not drinking it," he said.

"You're changing the subject."

"The cooker is worthy of a lengthy discussion."

The old man, who sold me the house, left the cooker. It is a pre-war Belling which is substantially enamelled, has Queen Anne legs, and toast takes thirty minutes. The oven works not badly at all. The hotplates take forever.

"Is that why you won't stay the night?" I said.

"No, it is because you are impossible and faddy."

"Faddy?"

"What did you eat last night?"

"Cheese and onion," I said. "You do like my home if not me?" The house, like the cooker, is older than I. There is a monkey-puzzle tree on the back lawn and built onto the rear is a sort of home-made conservatory with cane chairs. I have yet to get rid of the two baths in the front garden. There are wild hedges showing years of neglect and the paint must have started to peel before the Second World War.

"Are you on Welfare?" said Tomas.

"Can I claim Welfare?"

"Of course not."

"Why not? I can't afford a gardener and I work with my hands therefore I am working class. That must make me eligible for Welfare?"

"Working class? You've an eighteenth century bracket clock in your hall…"

"I haven't the staff to wind it, have I?"

"And a Jaguar and a Mini in your garage," said Tomas.

"Can't drive the fucking things, can I?"

"Your fault."

"Why?" I said.

"The Drunk in Charge?"

"Someone slipped me a Mickey Finn and I was incarcerated overnight – no en suite that was why I tried to urinate out the cell window. I told you this in confidence and now you are throwing it back in my face. You can be a very nasty bastard, Tomas."

I don't drive because I've lost my nerve. Lying to Tomas casts serious doubts on our relationship.

The kitchen door was open onto the lean-to. The fog had lifted and hailstones hammered the corrugated iron sheeting which provides a roof. Cosy. I enjoy sounds like that; wind in a chimney does it for me too. There are falls of soot from the hail. The chimneys need sweeping. I'll ask Tomas later. He'll do it, he's so capable.

"I think you are very wonderful doing my central

heating," I said.

"You need a new boiler. You want me to enquire?"

"Could you? I do think you're very wonderful."

"Shut up."

"I am facetious but it's my way of being sincere."

"So what do you think?" he said.

"I am thinking sex," I said, wondering if I could bring up the fact that the chimneys need sweeping.

"I am looking at empty crisp packets in the wastepaper basket? Cheese and onion? And you're not drinking your soup," he said, opening his fly, easing off his jeans.

"What I can't understand is why I am not working class when I have work tomorrow. Take off your top. It excites me." He rolled over, was face down on the settee, and with my fingers moving under his muscular body into hair, I said, "Do you know a good chimney sweep?"

"Wednesday evening? I've brushes. I think that the soot can be used on the garden? I'll check. I'll cook something," said Tomas.

I was so grateful he hadn't mentioned Deirdre. Deirdre heralds depression. He wouldn't mention her now I was inside him. I wouldn't come but he would and would be in a frenzy of passion, such is his need to have sex with men.

He came copiously and was apologising for the mess. When I told him it could be used on the garden, he loved that. Sex with me calms him.

Poor Deirdre. She doesn't know he loves men and only likes women.

WAYLAND

Youths from school usually put in for promotion straightaway. Promotion means actually reading the contents of the envelopes rather than sorting them. Wayland is an exception, a nineteen year old, who seems happy to stay in our department opening envelopes.

His hair is near enough black and his sensitive fingers could be those of a concert pianist. Pleasant enough but I thought little of him until we jammed together in the doorway to the washrooms and I automatically apologised. As my mind was elsewhere, I asked him to repeat what he had said.

"I said we must stop meeting like this. You like my hair?" he said.

"You've good hair, liked it better when you had it shorter, sort of more casual butch, you know?"

He is no way effeminate so I was wondering if I had put my foot in it and took the safest course and washed my hands whilst he sought sanctuary, perhaps, in a cubicle.

Naomi says he's drippy, so I asked Ginny what she thought of Wayland.

"He reminds me of a caged rat. Never still, darting about the small cage, desperately looking for a way out or a mate," said Ginny.

Wayland stares at me often with those hazel eyes. It is this intense observation of me which interests. He demands my company defiantly and has to attack me verbally, but he is without malice, it is his way of getting to know me.

He said, "You've been painting? Your hands? Filthy."

Acutely aware of each other, we examine the other. He is tall and slim, not skinny-slim though, and I note the large well shaped ears, the broad nose and the full lips and dark hairs soft on his cheeks. When he looks at me he is endearing… There is something vulnerable about him which is kind of nice.

With him I am liable to spill beans.

He visited the barbers yesterday and his thick hair is short all over, combed forward.

"Your hair looks good," I said.

He played the fool. "What? What? You want to smell my hair?"

"Do you want me to smell it?"

Wayland sniffed his armpit. "How about you smelling that?"

Wayland is now devoted to teasing me. He acts with me in a way he simply does not act with anyone else. Wayland is certain that he can get away with anything. The way he carries on has a lot to do with him being nineteen, and a lot to do with him knowing my sexual preference.

I ran into him again later that same morning.

"You are following me around," he said.

We were near the swing door which led out the office into a corridor busy with clerks and as I opened it, it was as if we were linked by an invisible thread, he tagged along. I was drinking from the water fountain, suspicious of the mouthpiece going green and wondering about others' germs, when I felt hands. I glanced down and there were sensitive fingers tight gripping either side of my waist. The fingers went. I stood. Wayland turned and opened the washroom door and waited for me. His gaze was solely on me, eyes so greenish brown.

My hands had paint on them so I had intended to wash them. Wayland went into a cubicle then came straight out and pointing at the urinals, said, "Can't use those."

"Piss in the cubicle and talk," I said. "I know how you feel. In the forces we flew to Malta from a military airport in Hampshire. A long queue of squaddies. Only one lavatory and ahead of me was a colonel peeing. He told me to come in and join him to speed up the queue."

Wayland said, "What did you do?"

"Waited until he had finished. Did you want me to join you?"

He flushed the lavatory, came stood by me. "You can tell me to wash my hands."

"Urine is a disinfectant. Some folk drink it."

"This colonel, why would he do that?" said Wayland.

"Real men do not have hangups about such things also he was showing me that he was one of the chaps when it came to pissing."

As I dried my hands on a paper towel Wayland talked animatedly about a man who works on another floor and whom he had seen waiting outside a notorious pickup lavatory in the park. The man was watching men go in and out.

"You were outside a public lavatory watching a man who was watching other men?" I said.

"What was he doing?"

"He was doing what you were doing." I threw a long-distance coarse damp paper towel nonchalantly into the wire basket, pleased when it went in. "You do know that public lavatories are trysting places for queers?"

"What places?" He shot back into his cubicle and shut the door.

I could easily make a move on him and Wayland would not be silly about it but instinct tells me that somehow it might be too soon.

The day of lurking homosexuality continued during my lunchtime walk. I paused outside the park lavatory, wondering if Wayland might visit it with cheese rolls and a flask of coffee to dine in a cubicle in an observatory way, taking notes to relay to me. I shuddered thinking about the lack of hygiene but lingered and watched a man go in and another come out. Then out slouched a nondescript young man with shoulder length dirty-blond hair. From the cut of his clothes, I guessed he was a foreign student, Northern European. He stared at me and unzipped and urinated hard against the brick wall, his gaze on me all the time, tongue moistening lips, then he masturbated at the side of the lavatory part-concealed by bushes, mouth open, pink tongue showing. I found his sperm arcing and hitting and hitting the brick wall erotic. Finished, head down, he hurried towards the college. I had missed out and my erection was urgent. My fly unzipped. And with no one watching, no audience to silently cheer me on, shamefacedly I ejaculated on the same wall. I had been timid in the stalls and was too late on stage.

I certainly could not talk about it to Tomas nor Salvatore. I made a beeline for someone with whom I would not feel guilt.

"Where? Where?" said Wayland in high excitement. I told him and he rushed out during his lunch break to return half an hour later to drag me from my desk into the privacy of the cloakrooms. And when we were sandwiched between rows of bulging hung-up coats, he said,

"And it was all up the wall." He was red faced and as excited as a child opening presents as he pressed his body to mine.

"Work," I said.

As we walked down the stairs instinct warned me not to get involved with him. He was too passionate, too dependent, and, "You like women best, don't you?" I said.

"Yes." He became shy, head down, eyes up.

"You didn't look, did you?" I was urging him to say no.

"Of course I looked because I like you. And we're walking hand in hand, Ralph?"

It was natural with him and I felt relaxed as I returned to my workplace where I chatted to Enid, her hair immaculate, her body heavy in middle-age. Well dressed. She makes the best of herself, Alice had said.

Enid, always on the ball, reminded me. "Your dental check up?"

"Shit!" I glanced at the clock. "*Ten* minutes?"

"He always runs late."

I scooted out the building, doubled to the town. Made it and was in the chair for only five minutes so afterwards I had time to shop in a department store.

On returning to the office I placed a bottle of Aramis in Wayland's drawer.

Back from tea and flushed with excitement, he rushed up to me. "For me?"

"My farewell gift."

"You're not leaving?" His hand hovered over mine.

"No, but our affaire de coeur is finished. I have a boyfriend."

"I don't know things, Ralph. When I ask Danny about sex, he says I must be kidding." Wayland looked sad.

I was surprised at the affection I felt for this young man as I held his hand; its sticky warmth reassuring in mine. Tugging him out into the corridor, I said, "I'm going to sort out the stationery locker. Come on?"

“Ralph, I want to know. Didn’t shave until I was seventeen. Didn’t wank either.”

“So you were late maturing. It happens.”

“I didn’t know anything about sex.”

In this day and age? Was Wayland serious?

I said, “School? Kids talk about stuff and… And the TV? There is a sex change programme on now?”

“My spine. In hospital off and on for seven years. Car accident. Both parents died. Live with Gran.”

“Go on?” I said.

“Gran never watches sex on TV. She is frail and has had a heart attack recently. A nurse comes in daily so mostly it’s me looking after her.”

We were in the narrow corridor which led to the stationery locker and he was still talking. “When I was seventeen I went into a public lavatory and a man was playing with himself. Didn’t know what he was doing but when I got home I tried it.”

I said, “I was eleven, maybe ten, when I first did it.”

“See? I need help. Naomi calls me drippy.”

“Naomi isn’t the only fish in the sea.”

He looked about to cry. “You’re a looker, Ralph, and the women fancy you and you don’t fancy them and women don’t fancy me.”

“That’s the perversity of life.”

“What’s that mean?”

“Life’s not easy for queers. You’re bisexual. Go for women.”

He blurted out. “But they don’t like me. Would you have sex with me if I was queer?”

“Try me,” I said. Wayland is not the hottest man in town, yet the eyes, the slim smooth body.

“That Aramis? You…?”

"I like you. No bribe, no ties, no obligations. Okay?"

"You can tell me things in the locker?" he said.

"I need help too," I said.

"I really like you because you don't try it on like Budd does," he said.

"I won't tell anyone what we talk about," I said.

"I want you to tell others that you and I had sex."

"You're saying we don't have sex and I tell people we have?"

"Naomi is jealous of me talking to you."

"You're using me as a trophy?" I said smiling.

"Naomi is gorgeous but she says I am thick and sexless. You talk to me. You tease me but that's in an okay way. What Naomi says makes me squirm."

Wayland looked happy as I unlocked the stationary locker door and when we went into the small oblong room lined with shelves, I said, "So it's no to sex. But yes to hypothetical sex? Will hypothetical oral sex do you?"

"What's oral sex?" he said.

I do wish he'd stop kidding me.

I touched his hard through his jeans.

"Show me the oral sex, Ralph?" His palm was damp on my face.

I locked the door. Undid his zip.

"You okay?" I said.

He nodded.

I knelt, pushed down his jeans, my hands smoothing his white legs, my fingers gentle between his thighs, touching the short hairs, cradling his tight scrotum and his urgent erection. I said, "Put your hands in my hair, communicate affection with touch." I looked up into his eyes. "You want affection or passion?"

As my mouth slid over his penis he was pumping and

wretched. I pulled him to the floor and nursed him tight to my chest. Holding him and talking to him to comfort him.

He said, "In the forces did you see many men's cocks?"

"Male jesting was manly in the communal shower but giggling stuff was a no-no. One married marine, who had everything going for him, told me that a queer had sucked him off. And another marine confessed he'd stayed with a queer in his Devon home. And in the heads graffiti advertised the lonely desperate for dates but I didn't cotton on. Thought them jokes. I weep at my naiveté."

Wayland undid my belt and his hand was gentle on my erection. Watching him, I came quickly. Wayland caught it in his hand and used it to rub his cock and I turned towards him as his seed pooled on my stomach.

When dressing he said, "What are those scars?"

"Nothing."

"Ralph?"

I took his hand and squeezed it until pain registered. "A bullet so stop asking questions." I was being too dramatic and silly. "It was in the forces. Want to forget about it."

As we tidied the shelves of stationery, we chatted and I felt close to him. Often, I find, sex distances.

He said, "The others know we have been doing it. No one has tried the door. Can I say we acted like animals? Danny will spread the word if I tell him that."

I kissed Wayland and we swayed together, fondling each other, wanting more. "Tell Danny but no details. You talk details and it is boasting and demeaning and get yourself a girl…"

"I like you…"

"My partner? Jealous. I can't split with him because he is an excellent plumber."

As I went to unlock the door, Wayland took hold of my

hand and pressing my palm to his lips, he kissed it.

Next morning I was thinking I'd best cool it with Wayland when I was told I had to take a telephone call in the chief executive's office with the chief executive, gaunt in clerical grey seated at his desk, openly listening.

The caller had a down to earth young voice, confident enough. I could almost grade him. He'd be bright, early twenties, being groomed for better things. "You're fluent in Russian and God knows how many other languages, Ralph?" He'd know, it was on my file from my time in the forces. Then came the flattery "Your first class mind and your track record have not been forgotten. The Israelis have been enquring?" I said, "I think not. I am happy as a filing clerk." My irony did not faze him, he said, "I know you are waiting for a phone to be installed at home. I will hurry the installation along and phone you Tuesday."

As I left, the chief executive said, "Any phone calls to make, Ralph, my door is open. I have his number."

Despite two Valium it took less than half an hour for the migraine to strike. It made life unbearable. If there were a self-destruct button, my finger would have been on it. For half an hour I sat on the lavatory, trousers up, tears running. I was desperate for sympathy and at lunch-break Naomi suggested we walk in the park, feed the swans, and as we sat on a bench I vomited then was apologising. She gave me two tablets. "Prescription only. Mum's." When back in the office, she had Wayland phone a taxi to take me home. Wayland stopped the afternoon with me. The tablets were taking effect so I confided, suggested the caller might be MI6 or GCHQ.

"What's GCHQ?" he said.

"Intelligence, codes, translating – stuff like that?"

"The Common Market?" he said.

I smiled and said he was beautiful.

"You need glasses, Ralph."

"Go out and make a phone call for me?"

Wayland read the installation advice I gave him, said, "You want I cancel the order for your telephone?" And when in the kitchen he was in the fridge. "You need milk and butter. And bread. I'll make a list."

I gave him a cheque and my driving licence, said, "Corner shop. Tessa will cash the cheque for Ralph. And two bottles of Teachers."

I fell asleep and woke as Wayland was positioning a mug of tea and a substantial plate of sandwiches on a low table near me.

"Cancelled your phone. Got you cheese and loads of tinned stuff and some brilliant ham. Rang Gran. Said I'd be a bit late." He knelt by me, his long fingers, red with the cold, were cooling on my forehead and my migraine was fading. I was wanting him as he said, "Gotta go 'cos my bus is in ten minutes otherwise Gran worries. Got her some of that ham." His hand was on mine. "Wish I could stay and sleep with you. Cuddle you when you wake up, make you feel better."

NAOMI AND HAMISH

Stamping the mountains of filing is so mindlessly repetitive that I understand the tedium of factory work. One rare act, requiring thought, is to change the date in the rubber stamp. The other week one clerk stamped several hundred documents the fourteenth instead of the fifteenth. He had to amend them all by hand.

Enid and I stopped working to listen to the shouting match between Naomi and the supervisor.

"I want that trollop off this table," said Enid. "Have you seen her neck? She's sitting on a fortune."

But Naomi, love bites and all, was staying in the end seat so she could be kept under the supervisor's eye.

I said to her, "You permanently with us?"

Her face was red with fury as she glared at Enid. "God, I hope not even though I do love you desperately, Ralph darling. I want off this table because of you know who."

Enid blushed and hurried to the restaurant leaving me with Naomi whose desk is covered in angry ink blotches, there is a pinned-up picture of Sid Snot and three soft drink bottles all part full. A half eaten cake is in her drawer. "I am waiting for the mould to grow," she had told me.

"I like you here," I said.

"You're a liar but a very sexy liar."

"Trouble is, with your looks, no male can look at you without thinking of sex."

"God, Ralph!" She hid her face in her hands.

I stood over her. "Except me. I am different."

"Wayland was on about you? Didn't believe him."

I said nothing.

"I get on your nerves lusting after you?" said Naomi.

"You don't. You know you're safe with me. That's my attraction. You are the sophisticate who plays her heartless cruel games," I said.

"But with Wayland?"

I said, "He and I were animals."

I never dreamt I could say that and not howl with laughter, but Naomi said, "I can see it in your face. Do you do it with Hamish?"

I shook my head.

She said, "Hamish is sweet. I adore him. He doesn't go with women but he loves my anger. Ginny's been complaining that he's lazy and smokes during a no-smoking period. Have you seen how many she smokes?"

Hamish's mouse-coloured hair is lazily long and sits limply on the collar of his green shellsuit; he has recently grown a startling moustache. This is Hamish quietly two fingering authority. He will be taken aside by management and he will promise to change his clothes and he will come in wearing acceptable smart jeans for a week then there will be another outrageous outfit.

Hamish is younger than I and he can be private about his sexuality but it is sort accepted between us that we are two of a kind. I mean, as I waited in the washroom for him to finish peeing, I said, "I like to watch cocks." Then laughing, we strolled back into the office.

When I sat down, Enid whispered over the desktop, "His hair needed attention last year. And that moustache?"

"Yucatán," I said.

"The shellsuit again? It will be mentioned."

"It sure will."

"His cigarettes have saltpetre in them. And he's been getting hot water for free. I shall be having a word in someone's ear about that," said Enid.

I got on with my work until the supervisor stormed up to Hamish, shouting, "I saw you! I saw you! You can buy hot water for a penny in the restaurant."

I questioned Naomi about hot water usage in the office and she explained that the coffee vending machine in the corridor squirts hot water into a cardboard cup which contains a dispensed instant yuk coffee and milk powder. Hamish has been using this hot water – which is free – for his own instant coffee instead of following office instructions and buying his hot water for one penny in the restaurant.

I said, "You have to be fucking kidding me?"

Naomi loves me swearing when it gets an eavesdropping Enid fuming.

Enid said, "The penny is for the Welfare Fund."

"There's over twenty thousand pounds in the Welfare Fund and it is for the welfare of staff. The penny is typical of this place. Petty and parochial."

"He could bring his hot water from home in a Thermos," said Enid.

"That stupid comment pisses me off," I said.

When Enid came back from her break, her claws had been sharpened. "I've heard that Budd is coming to this floor and is going to sit next to Wayland."

I said nothing.

Enid had the talons out all right. "Perhaps you'd like to sit next to Wayland for a change?"

I had had a thank you card. It was written with a touching sincerity *Happiness for always, with all my love to you, Wayland.* I said to Enid, "Sure. Love the guy." Wayland is without malice or prejudice and sure as hell he wouldn't know how to be snide and carp.

Enid was horrified and open-mouthed at my somewhat over the top declaration. Made brave from confrontation, her sensible shoes trod where such heterosexual shoes should fear to tread. Her eyebrows were raised, indignation reddened her interfering nose.

"Have you ever considered a normal life? Marriage?"

"Normal is ranting and raving about not paying a penny

for hot water? This place is a nursing home for the mentally crippled with its belly-aching women and cobwebbed men who have risen from the grave."

Enid stared at me in disbelief. "Have you been drinking?"

I took out my flask and took a long pull. "Want one?"

"And your language," said Enid. "Don't worry. I won't report you."

"Go ahead, being a sneak suits you."

Salvatore ambled alongside me on my way to the bus stop, his head bent listening.

I said, "Hamish's problem is he isn't cute. It's bullying because he's queer."

"How did your fine mind work out that?"

"Figure it. Take Daniel. Daniel is young, irreverent, rude, plays the most outrageous pranks. No one picks on him."

"They pick on Naomi," he said.

"Naomi is female so she's fair game. Naomi bitches about them and is better at it. Daniel is male. Daniel is sex to them. I am surprised that your fine mind hasn't sussed that out," I said.

"They don't pick on you because you have a sign about your neck saying *I am gorgeous and I fuck men so fucking what?*"

"That is outrageous, you Dago shit," I said in Italian. Not my best language but it gave my words bite and had sexy Salvatore replying in Italian.

"Dago is Hispanic not Italian."

"It can be both to the illiterate bigots such as I," I said.

"They pick on Hamish because he's different. You're a

smoothie, sexy and liked – though God knows why. You're the same as them. You only like me because you fancy me."

In Italian I said, "Salvatore, you're the hottest thing in town. And I love you because you talk the language of passion."

"You're a devious bastard," he said.

I slipped my hand in his, and Salvatore being Salvatore, gripped it and we walked hand in hand until we reached the bus stop where I said, "Isn't this marvellously Latin?"

"You went over the top with Enid. If you hate the place – leave." Looking at the watching bus queue, he said, "You're going to kiss me, aren't you?"

"No, I respect you too much to embarrass you. And I will apologise to Enid." He was beaming until I added, "Fifty quid for anal sex? You passive."

Getting off the bus at my stop, alone and lonely without the company of Salvatore, I drank two cold pints in *The Six Lanes* which is an over-large, chilly thirties public house with a great deal of red brick and few customers. Tried to phone Tomas but two public phones were out of order and the third was coated in vintage vomit. Bought a bottle of scotch and went home to watch television. Chilled in the armchair at three in the morning I jerked awake from a nightmare of spurting blood and voices.

I had the hangover from hell as I boarded the first bus of the day which is a single decker which usually carries the same passengers to work but the driver changes. The driver today was Punk, dark haired with flea runs and he is mid twenties. Hugely sexy. Glorious muscular arms. I drool as he drives as if the bus were a sports car. Punk put his foot down. Slip-road ahead warned a sign. We did seventy, eighty. I shut my eyes and my hangover had me praying for a quick death and I would be in heaven with the lusted-after Punk. The journey of eight miles took ten minutes. With two stops? I'd have to check my timing.

The Major, to whom I say good morning and little else, looked at me as we approached our stop and said,

"Perhaps he'll open the doors and we'll roll out?"

I lingered and, still drunk, grasped Punk's muscular arm before leaving the bus. "You're quite something."

"Thought you'd enjoy the thrill," he said huskily.

I was almost dribbling sex as I limped off the bus. Why the hell can't I say what I mean? I fancy you like crazy and I want sex with you now. But in these days of so called liberation if he is straight he'd punch me or tell me to get fucked. I could be impugning his virility and Punk has loads of that.

In the office, I prayed we would not suffer more Hamish dramas as I patted him on the back to say good morning and he turned and smiled and everything was all right until he helped himself to Nora's newspaper. For eighteen years Nora has read her *Daily Express* at her break but today Hamish has taken it. Anyone but Nora.

Nora and Enid were in cahoots.

"Well, he can't do that too often!" Enid was at her most Enid-ish when she shared her own newspaper with Nora with whom she rarely speaks.

"And he's been taking Sarah's tissues *again,*" said Ginny.

All the time Hamish sat reading the *Express,* sipping coffee made from free hot water. I swivelled in my chair, banged him in the ribs, pointed at the newspaper, mouthed, "Give!" and nodded towards a seething Nora. He laughed and handed her the newspaper and took a pile of work up to the typing pool.

There is a new man who sits opposite Ginny, and he raised the Venetian blind, to some applause, while Hamish was out of the office, knowing that Hamish has a problem with his eyes and cannot tolerate direct sunlight.

Naomi strode over to him. "Close the blind and try being a decent human being." Her voice flat and deadly, her face red with anger as she said to the new man who was fixed in his chair, "What're you doing this evening?" Naomi wasn't suggesting a date.

"Nothing." The new man stuttered.

"This evening Hamish is manning a telephone advising callers about AIDS."

There was a terrible hush. The new man obediently dropped the blind. Ginny sat open mouthed, not speaking. I think all of us were learning a lesson in humility from a dizzy nineteen-year-old who dreams through the day or suffers bouts of fury against the establishment. This dark, sultry young woman stood over me and sighed.

I said, "I wish I had your style."

"I wish we were having sex." Her thigh-tight jeans rested on my shoulder.

"I am sulking and furious with myself," I said.

"The sex, Ralph?"

"I am quite happy daydreaming of my Scandinavian houseboy – Olaf Boghandle." I was thinking about Punk the sexiest bus driver ever.

"Ralph darling, do you feel drawn towards Sid Snot physically?"

I stood, kissed her hair and she held my hand tight.

Naomi had sorted it. I've always had respect for the power of women.

DANIEL AND FREDDIE

Daniel is one of The Young.

Daniel has a perfect English complexion, he could appear on soap adverts. He misses out on being the teenage dream in other directions: his jeans are well past their sell by date and the trainers are grey from scuffing on his motorbike, his t-shirts are mostly a horrid orange but he gets away with the ghastly t-shirts and walks in the manner of someone who knows he looks good.

Daniel approves of me and Wayland having sex and considers me to be an honorary member of The Young for when we pass each other there is an acknowledgement. His "All right then?" is kind of Masonic.

Daniel and I bumped into each other as I pushed aside the concertinaed coats to hang up my jacket on a sliding metal hanger.

Close to he isn't nice-looking. His perfect complexion was reddened by the wind. It was as if a masterpiece had been taken off a wall and shoved in my face and I had lost perspective and all I could see were daubs of paint.

"All right then?" said Daniel as he left me, pushing through the heavy swing door. His legs were far too long and his arms bony.

But tailing him into the office at a distance I see what the artist wants me to see, the burst of young life and the henna catching the light in his glorious hair.

The Daniel portrait was back on the Louvre wall.

He had left a pile of filing near me so I returned it.

He said, “That’s old Bateman’s work.” He pointed to the beak-nose grey haired Bateman. “Stinks he does. I tell him he stinks.” When Daniel speaks there is a nervous edge to his voice and I wonder if it is only me who can see that beneath the beautiful exterior he is flinching. He said, “When Bateman rubber-stamps, he’s a fucking pile-driver, that’s the MasterBates-man Sound. I tell him. I say, ‘MasterBates-man you stink!’ And he goes mad. Watch.”

Daniel carried the pile of work across to Bateman whose little finger was stuck up a nostril. Daniel, young and wholesome in body-slim clothes, grinned at Bateman. Daniel’s perfect lips, and strong young teeth, contrasted to Bateman’s gaping mouth as Bateman held up his head to listen to Daniel.

Daniel said, “Your breath smells.”

Bateman was visibly annoyed. He blew air out of his mouth like a puffer train.

Daniel said to me, “Listen to him. He’ll go spare.” Then he turned to Bateman, said, “New talent show on ITV. You’d win it. It’s for the foulest breath ever.”

The gaping mouth clamped shut, the tilted head went back a little further, then the puffing stopped. “All right, you nasty specimen. I shall leave. I shall leave now!”

There was none of the dignity that Bateman strove for as he stalked away leaving the dishy Daniel laughing, lolling on the table.

I cannot like Bateman. Mouth agape, laboured speech and he is constantly rolling something in his fingers. “We all know where that came from,” Enid had said.

Daniel gets away with this kind of play-ground cruelty because he is attractive. Were it to happen the other way around, were Bateman to tell Daniel that his breath stank when it does not, that would be a different cup of halitosis.

I got to wondering how shy Daniel really is after he told me how he was caught in a man's house. A man who works in the office.

"That woman he lives with came in when he had my front undone," he said.

Testing him, wanting him, I invited him out. He was shocked, hurried away but I caught his arm. I had gone too far. I am certain that he doesn't bother with any other man. Daniel likes girls.

I disappeared to have a cigarette in the lavatory and returning felt better seeing Daniel smiling.

"Why are you sitting opposite me?" I said.

His eyes alive, his head moving with an almost imperceptible jerk as Daniel waited a moment before explaining. "Enid's helping them out and they…" He nodded at the formidable Alice and her cronies at the other end of the office "…said I smell."

He seemed a child, ready to talk nonsense but enjoying his physical beauty I smiled at him. He held out a hand.

"Do you want to hold hands?" I said.

Danny will take none of my nonsense, he's no push-over like Wayland. "Give me your work. I am putting mine away."

Danny left for home at the same time as I, and we walked together to the exit where he told me that the man who said, Goodnight to us was the man who had opened his front.

Freddie.

Because the work is so factory-like a certain amount of noise is tolerated. Freddie goes over the top, he imitates animals and he sings.

I said to Enid, "When he was stamping his filing this morning, we had...?"

"*Colonel Bogey…*"

"*Lillibullero* and I think I caught some Bizet?" I said.

"With percussion," said Enid, "You can't see from your seat but when he reaches out for the cymbals… A treat."

She went for coffee and missed Freddie standing for ten minutes making the telephone engaged signal.

I don't hold grudges so Enid and Ginny and I had declared a truce after the Hamish brouhaha. She and Ginny had told me that some years back Freddie had had one hell of a breakdown.

Today Freddie confessed to me that last week he had driven to Tilbury docks.

"I parked near a big boat with a black funnel. Ralph, I wanted to get on board, get a job. A few hundred yards separated me from freedom. I am thirty-six. I've got to do something before it's too late."

The running away days to sea were long gone… but maybe there was a chance? A ship flying a flag of convenience would not be too scrupulous. So why didn't he board the ship and *ask*? I know why, because I know how he felt. I said, "Try Tilbury again? I'll come with you?"

His "Thanks, me old mate" was phonily butch and at odds with the cologne and the fashion clothes. He said, "Don't forget I'm giving you a lift home Friday?"

He had missed out on a chance to escape in Tilbury. I mean, giving me a lift is a way of him saying he wants sex with me. Sex with me is not going to help him get a life.

On Friday I caught the early morning single decker which is old and smelt of San Izal. The major and the nice guy from the greengrocers in town were the only other passengers. Punk stopped on the narrow bridge near the *The Sloop* and pointed downstream towards the sea. A heron was standing in the shallows. As we neared Landrose with its rustic bus stop and village green Punk slowed because a rabbit was running in front of the bus.

The man from the greengrocers shouted, "Bloody nature tour. Give it a red flag." Then after five minutes, he said, "Myxomatosis. Run it down, mate. It's humane."

"Don't look like myxomatosis to me," said Punk.

It was riveting. The rabbit was stuck on course and we followed at a rabbit's pace until we reached my stop. The major widened his eyes at me in comment as he got off.

As the rabbit headed for a hedge, I said to Punk, "Loved it."

"Knew you would, you being the sensitive type."

"Meaning me being queer?" I would chance my arm when sex with him could be remotely on the cards.

A slow long look at me. "Your last ride with me. I got a job at the airfield."

"You can't leave me!"

"Leave you?"

"You heard!"

Even though his acne scarred face was impassive; his small dark eyes were examining me then came a slow grin.

"It's a proper job. Management but mostly instructing. Parachuting."

"I jumped in the forces. Had to wear nappies," I said.

"I'm impressed. You hang out in Bourgeois Boulevard – same like me. You're the sagging detached screaming for attention? Looks like squatters have abandoned it?"

"You're the cute terrace with the grotesque ghastly green gnomes?"

"You into alliteration?" he said.

The guy who worked in the greengrocers had had enough. "For Christ's sakes some of us have to work!"

Punk, winking at me, said, "See you in *Noel's?* Midday? Skydiving would open your bowels again?"

"It'd open my fly."

"Bring tissues – man-sized." Then those sensational muscular arms were doing their job, driving the bus, driving me mad with lust.

God, he was the most exciting man. Sad faced, I stood lonely on the pavement as the single decker burnt rubber as it sped off in a farewell to me.

Flexitime had me finishing work for the week well before lunch, and Freddie had his hand on my shoulder as he steered me between the rows of tables and past tins brimming files, towards the exit. There had been something deliberately casual about his invitation to give me a lift although it had been brewing all week.

"No bother, kid. No bother at all. Going to your neck of the woods this Friday. A good hardware shop there; thin on the ground these days."

Through overhead branches, lush with early summer greenery, sunlight fell in patches on the narrow asphalt road. Freddie raised his hand to salute people he does not know. When an oncoming motorist stopped to let him through, he said to the motorist, who couldn't hear, "Oh, that is very, very nice of you."

His suck up to other drivers got me tense.

He said, "The Head Girl told me, mate, that your sexual tastes lie in other directions."

This was outrageous. I have never been closeted at work while closeted Freddie had wanted cock and had exploited Daniel's friendship to rip open his front and be caught doing it, and now Freddie was giving his blessing to my homosexuality.

As we were entering the narrow congested High Street, I said, "If you're serious about going to sea, I know someone who might help. You want me to try?"

"How about me buying you a few ales and lunch? I can leave the car, get a taxi home?"

He wasn't interested. He was a dreamer, doomed. I said, "I've got an appointment."

Freddie shook hands and thanked me for my company then drove off.

Poor Freddie, so polite, so wanting sex, so forgetful – forgetting to visit the hardware store.

PART TWO – UNIFORMS

PUNK

I spotted Punk reading a notice in the window of a small novelty shop. I went to catch up with him but he deliberately walked on, turning to stare at me. I think his glare was meant to be an encouraging smile. Reading the notice would delay me but it was a must: a handwritten postcard which advertised the *Trucker Club* which was featuring on Saturday *Want to Spunk* which I imagined to be a pop group rather than an invitation to a community event.

It excited me to tail Punk sexy in a black t-shirt tight at a butch neck. I lusted after his Adam's apple and his slim hips in those black fitted jeans. His face, with its small alert brown eyes, is incredibly appealing.

My wild man Punk ain't wild at all, he lives at home with mummy and daddy. I've seen his father in a suit and his mother's makeup is carefully tended as are the neat curtains in their terrace home.

He crossed the road and turned to look at me for a second time. He was shy! As a bus driver he had been in control but now… I stuck out my tongue and he laughed and dropped his newspaper. Pages blew about the pavement. My next door neighbour, waiting at the bus stop, helped him gather them.

He thanked her politely and as I approached he extended his hand. I held it, not shaking it but holding it firmly. He delicately moved his fingertips over my palm. That sent urgent messages to my groin.

"Finished with the buses. I'm off the sauce tomorrow, need a clear head. You up for a jump? This Sunday?" The tip of his tongue moistened his pink lips.

I was very aware of Punk's erotic grasp and aware that Margaret, my neighbour, would be wondering why we were holding hands and wondering what the Sunday jump could entail.

"A pint at *Noel's?*" he said, studying me.

"Half an hour do you?"

"Noel attracts all the weirdos," he said.

"That's me classified?"

Big smile. "I am meeting Victor, he works in your office?"

"I know Vic." Victor is an actor who lives his life

playing the role of the definitive queen. 'I am a pantomime dame for the boring straights amusement, Ralph.'

"Got to shower, make a phone call if you is up for it?" A business card was in my hand, a scowl at me and he was gone, doubling along the pavement. He paused to shout, "Make it an hour!"

"Isn't it boiling?" Margaret's silk blouse plunged showing a reddish chicken neck.

I nodded politely but the north-westerly was decidedly chill. She was too young for the change unless having me as a neighbour had brought it on prematurely.

"We're going to have to move," she said.

"Real sorry about that."

"The street. Not the same."

It is a street of mostly detached houses in landscaped grounds with double garages and radio controlled gates. There is a line of architect designed terrace houses with cute gardens and as she watched Punk roll towards one, she said, "He's a nice enough lad, I suppose, but it used to be accountants and lawyers and Mr Finch who had your place was in the Foreign Office but now they've built the estate the street's full of cleaning ladies."

I wish to God it were. I would hire several immediately. I said, "Where's your car?"

"My darling is fixing it; fingers crossed. Hate buses," she said. "You haven't driven since you lost Plié, have you?" Her hand was sympathetically rubbing mine. "Seeing him had me weak at the knees. If you ever feel like talking, Ralph?"

I managed a smile and headed for my house.

Her talk of Plié and the thought of a Sunday jump had me swallowing a large scotch as soon as I was indoors.

Looking at a photograph had me swallowing another two. Then thinking about meeting Punk got me relaxed.

The English spring is like a sulky child breaking into thunder and drenching those of us who are foolish enough to venture out.

"A cutting wind which reflects my disposition," I said.

"Let's get inside before we're blown out to sea by your wit," said Tomas.

The thick concrete wall is a barricade against the sea; it is topped by a promenade and a broad road. Waves sometimes hit the wall and rise fifteen feet or so, and shingle is hurled up and over the road. Mortar in recently built houses is eaten away, substantial Victorian dwellings are crumbling and their gardens barren. On a corner, on the sea side of the promenade, sits *Noel's Bar* which is shielded from the weather, to some extent, by cliff.

Tomas led the way into *Noel's* where I perched on a barstool that rocked until I put beer mats under one leg. A fan heater was directed at me.

"He in a sulk again?" Noel said, nodding at Tomas who was frowning at his Coke.

I raised my eyes in an affirmative and said to Tomas, "You okay, lover?"

He ignored me so I tried to cheer him up, "You *Want to Spunk* this weekend?"

"What?" Tomas glowered at me but despite getting increasingly unsettled by his black moods, I breezed on: "Spunk is lisping slang for Punk who I lispingly lust after. When you revert from your perverted heterosexuality, that is get back to normal or abnormal, as society sees us, you and I will make an outstanding couple. We can discuss literature with plums in our mouths during the lads-excuse-me at the *Trucker Club* where *Want to Spunk* are appearing on Saturday."

"How many of those have you had?" he said.

I am okay with flashes of bad temper, I have them often but they last minutes not hours like the lingering moods of hate Tomas plunges into when... "You're seeing Deirdre this weekend?" I said.

"Claustrophobic in a cunting canal boat. Deirdre's best friend is bringing The Fiancée. If The Fiancée asks me if I fancy a double wedding, I'll smash his teeth in and if fat Phoebe goes on about the wedding all the way there and back, she'll be out the car and I'll piss on her." He held up his soft drink. "I'm driving. Two hours of it." His hand shook when lighting a cigarette.

"Hey, Tomas? You've got to talk to Deirdre, tell her you're bisexual. Women often guess, you know? You want I come with you?" I put my arm about his shoulders. He shoved it off as though he loathed me.

Noel glanced sympathetically at me and moved away.

"All I need is you acting camp."

"I would not act camp," I said.

"And what the fuck do you know about any fucking thing other than your fucking self?" said Tomas.

"Tomas, you stop this?"

"You are a superficial selfish lazy bullshitting bastard."

"Stop it!"

"Stop what? You get me to do all your DIY and then fuck every man that walks, cunt!" He drew phlegm from his lungs and spat it wet and sliding on my face.

My hands gripped his neck. He has no idea about self defence. I was giving him every chance. I was deliberately wide open waiting for an attacking move from him then I would counter. I wanted that move so I could… I stood back from him but still gripped his neck, saw his sudden comprehension of my power over his life in his eyes. It was terror. I had seen that terror before.

I let go of him as Punk's arm was tight about my waist then he was wiping my face with a tissue. "Weather's crap but the forecast is ace for Sunday, Ralph. Get your incontinence pants on. Victor is skydiving in sling-backs and surprising us in tulle."

A coughing Tomas was looking at me with scared eyes.

"You all right, darling?" said Victor, putting a scotch in front of me, ignoring Tomas.

"Thanks, Vic." I felt very ashamed.

We all fell silent as the wind shook the building. It was as if the pub was slightly drunk. Two glasses teetered on the bar counter and we watched as they rolled unbroken to the floor. After the roar of wind came silence.

"This pub is listed in the guide book as a folly. That right, Noel?" said Punk.

The wind then got up again and was buffeting the building. The door banged open as the storm gusted black over a violent sea.

As it slammed shut I could hear myself saying to Punk, "Let's you and me get out of here and go to Valparaiso?"

"We are jumping Sunday, Ralph."

"Don't know if I can. I didn't lose it then, did I?"

Tomas said, "You fucking lost it. Like you lost it when you pissed in a police cell."

As I lunged at him like a street brawler, Punk grabbed me about my chest.

"The bog now!"

Punk pulled me out of the bar, leaving Tomas harvesting his hate.

A maverick shaft of sunlight had the spotless Gents warm and cosy like a ship's heads. Outside chucked-up pebbles crashed against the reinforced window.

"Sorry about that." I blew my nose.

"You were scary. In control before but you did lose it when you tried to punch him," said Punk.

"What's your real name?" I said.

"Punk makes a statement."

"What statement? That you're my partner?"

"Your partner is Tomas."

"Dream on. You witnessed the schism. You're too old to be a punk?"

"Twenty-five? And I've got flea runs," he said.

"You're sexy as hell. Real good to look at. Lose the flea runs – pathetic at your age. They are part of a uniform saying *I am a punk* when you are not a punk," I said.

"Don't understand why your boyfriend fell out with you." He squeezed my erection through my jeans.

"Do that again and you can have my Jaguar. I'll throw in my body too – if you want it?"

He grinned, "You can't go back in the bar with that sticking up."

"Do something about it?"

"Victor says I'm butch but disabled by my genes. What's that mean?"

"It means you and I have sex."

Punk was at the urinal. He is five-five-ish, his amazing chest must be forty-four inches; his muscular arms attacked denim sleeves. "Warm, innit?" He shook it, quickly showed me it, and with a grin, zipped up, said, "Don't move" and was gone to reappear a few minutes later with a shot of whisky in a glass. "Tomas is near tears. I told him you would talk to him later."

"We're finished." I drained the glass, said, "I'll show you my dream home this evening?"

Big smile from him. "Garden by Capability Crap and them hedges what you got – reach for the sky. Blocked guttering that spews water and two baths rusting in the front garden and an old queen indoors eating cake but Versailles it ain't."

"How about you and me and cocktails and canapés in my conservatory at nine? If you don't come I shall be alone, slumped in a rattan chair, an empty gin bottle sad on the cold tiled floor, my breath stinking of booze, my hand moving stickily as I dream of you," I said, "Can you put up with me, Punk?"

"Slow down. First things first? Sunday? Brilliant mate owns the airfield. You and me are jumping together."

"Jumping? You're so exciting I can't walk."

Punk slowly undid my top shirt button, then the second button, then the third. "Nicest body hair outside of Naples. Are we going to be okay, Ralph?"

"Don't think I'll ever be okay."

"I'm serious about you but I'm not going behind your mate's back. I talk to him first," said Punk.

"Behind his back? Jesus Christ! Our parting was not amicable."

"He's got a problem and so have you. He wanted to kill you and you were scary. Needs sorting, mate. Needs sorting bad."

I opened my wallet, took out the wings which had been sewn on Plié's uniform. "These belonged to my soul mate. He and I trained together."

Punk gave me a tissue. I blew my nose.

"How about you helping instruct the newbies this Sunday?" he said.

"Newbies? Who the fuck says newbies?"

"Check your dictionary. I'll run through the how with you, see how it goes Sunday? You on?"

I undid my zip. "If I don't get rid of this, I'll spray walls."

"This is important. A wank is a wank. Transport is my Triumph Thunderbird," he said.

"We go in my car? You driving?"

"The Jag? You weren't joking? Drunken driving?"

"I lied to Tomas. Can't tell people that I lost my nerve, can I?" I said.

"Tell me about Tomas?"

"This weekend he is in a canal boat with his girlfriend. Weddings are the main course. Never seen fury like his. He really wanted to kill me. Why? I like him."

He said, "Being a bus driver I judge people as they step on board. You wouldn't have run down that rabbit, Tomas would."

"I had tests in the forces. A psychiatrist said I was a killer. Give me a hand-job and I'll jump Sunday?"

He stood alongside me at the window, his hand gentle in mine. "Them waves come in curling white. Watch the lower part of the wave foaming, going brown as the pebbles and sand are sucked up in the shallows."

The wave hurled pebbles high up the sea wall.

His lips were soft on mine, his hands eased my jeans down and, as he touched it I came and I was bent double, my mouth on his as we clung together.

"That isn't telling me that you wants Valparaiso," he said.

"Can we sneak out and escape to my house?"

"No, we cannot! Victor is my friend. We don't leave Vic." He gently dried me as I rested my forehead on his shoulder then I zipped up as he rubbed at the damp on his jeans, saying, "That'll get the message across."

I trailed him back into the bar where, made brave by two pints, I went outside to drop the iron shield over the lavatory window. Punk came to keep an eye on any curling wave that came in brown, for it was "Them breaking brown waves what hurls pebbles like a Gatling gun."

"You're a better man than I, Gunga Din," said Noel when we were back inside again after having got drenched.

"Ralph and me were playing at being butch. He's brilliant at it, I am crap," said Punk his face alive with laughter then he whispered to me, "I'll have a word with Tomas, the guy's hurting."

"Jesus…"

Punk raised his voice. "Victor, talk to Ralph, he's missing the office."

"So brave, Ralph darling," said Victor, making futile attempts to dry me by dabbing me with paper serviettes.

Punk took Tomas' arm, whispered in his ear and led him to the far end of the bar counter.

Victor waved his hand to order drinks, and handed Noel his own rapidly emptied peg glass for a refill, whispered to me, "Punk is solid gold."

Tomas and Punk were talking earnestly, not looking at me.

Victor was saying, "And that young Wayland? A lovely lad. Never stops talking about you. You are lucky."

"I'll pay for this round. You think I'm too promiscuous, Vic?"

"You are promiscuous, the 'too' is irrelevant, darling. You and Tomas must come back to my humble abode?"

Victor looked at Punk and sighed. "Punk cuts my hair. At least he's good for something. He's no oil painting, that's for sure. That shipwrecked face has sucked a thousand sailors." He addressed Punk, "Has my little butch boy got his scissors?"

Punk answered with two fingers.

Noel said, "Vic, you look like a camp Kamikaze pilot in that jacket."

A delighted Victor paraded in his white silk wind-breaker which had on the back a large red and blue eagle.

"I'd never dare wear this to work. Ralph is going to. So brave."

"I am putty in your hands, Vic," I said.

There is something so normal about Victor, camp as Christmas but something so normal about Victor as he said to Punk, "Do not expect me to carry the lunch, I'll faint!"

"Men do not carry shopping bags." Punk picked a raffia bag off the floor, winked at me.

Outside, bent double, battling against the fury of the wind, Tomas glanced shyly at me as we followed Victor and Punk to the pink Mini.

Tomas in front, and me in the back with Punk gloriously close.

I said, "Are me and Tomas still killing each other?"

Punk held up a low finger to silence me.

But Tomas was concentrating on Victor's driving as the car headed for the roundabout, mounted it and bumped over rough grass to bump off the other side. Tomas had been on soft drinks and was now sensible.

"Hairy, Vic? Best I drive?"

"Sorry, but I had to avoid that madman."

There were no pedestrians. Clouds of hammering white spray kept them off the promenade. The force of the storm was alarming. Victor must have lost control of the car in a violent gust.

"How many have you had?" said Tomas.

Punk made the sign of the cross.

"And I've the most garish lightweight sweater for Ralph to wear Monday," said Victor. "Return it in mint condition but I welcome certain stains. For lunch I've a lovely surprise waving frantically in the bag. And a divine fudge ice cream to follow. Ralph, wear a fur to work? To please me?"

"Am I to dress to outrage?" I said, thankful now we had turned onto a minor road leading into countryside.

"Darling, you shall go to the ball! A stole given me while doing *Peter Pan*. I'd rush to the front of the stage to ask the audience if they believed in fairies…"

Punk yawned.

"No to the fur, Victor," I said.

"Try it. Long and white – where have I heard *that* before? We can have a girls' afternoon."

"We'll be having a boys' funeral if you don't keep your eyes on the road," said Punk.

I was very aware of Punk's thigh hard pressing mine when he tapped Tomas' shoulder with one hand and held my hand with the other as he said, "You best tell Ralph?"

Tomas hung over the seat. I went beetroot, Tomas didn't, he said, "I'm going to ask Deirdre to marry me." I was dumbstruck. Tomas turned away but Victor was smiling encouragement at us.

Tomas grabbed the wheel and his fury at his sexuality had him screaming at Victor. "Stop the fucking car! Fucking stop the fucking car!"

As we skidded to a halt, Punk said cheerfully, "Take your hand off my fly, Ralph, I am not doing it in public."

"You always like this? I am sweating like a sauna."

"Tonight get the drawbridge lowered," Punk whispered, then studying Tomas, "Not hard to look at is he?" Then with voice raised, "It's them what's for us meal, Victor?"

"Lobster thermidor, darling."

"You want me to boil the poor little beggars?"

"So butch. Sings *The Eton Boating Song* at reunions. Tomas, slow here, my darling, then a right after the bridge. And I've only had *three* pints."

"With doubles. And them two pints with them whisky chasers in the *Barley Mow* and four of them tablets you take for your nerves…" said Punk.

"*Four?* Are you sure, darling?" Victor rattled his bottle of tablets at Tomas who stopped the car to study the label before saying, "Best put your feet up while I ring the chemists. Can they get an ambulance up this lane?"

"But the lunch?" said Victor.

"I'll cook lunch," said Tomas.

"But lobster thermidor, dear? It is lobster thermidor?"

Tomas parked in the lee of the thatched cottage which stood in isolation surrounded by fields. I felt relief. The din of the storm had gone. And Tomas was my boyfriend no more and I was with Punk who said, "You know how much skydiving could set you back? For you nothing. Long talk with Graham on the phone. He likes the sound of you and wants you in. The deal is for you to set up the new office then be management. Buy in, if you want? Real exciting, you and me and Graham who is lovely."

"He's not a *loads of money* freak?"

"Not! Graham rejected a buyout which would mean hard surfacing and lengthening the runway for a full commercial operation and have Graham retiring to a paradise island."

Victor, opening the car door, said, "Punk, you will transport the crustaceans and keep the nasty little cunts away from me. Tomas, your sturdy arm for me to lean on. Are you used to cooking with bottled gas? I had a very nasty blow-back last Tuesday."

I was relaxed left alone with Punk in the car.

He said, "I'm to stop at Graham's place two or three nights a week, help get the place sorted. You okay hanging on in at the office for a few weeks?"

"Can't I come with you?"

"I'll be popping back to see you."

When he said that I realised how serious we were.

THE OFFICE

The babble stopped. I saw why. A grey-haired cadaver was talking to a woman who must be a civic dignitary because she wore the kind of hat that only mayoresses and women at weddings have the arrogance and lack of taste to wear.

I am ignoring my work and am scribbling this. At the end of our table sits Salvatore yawning; his black stubble is nearing a beard, there are small red pimples of a rash on his cheeks, his good dark eyes are red-rimmed, the film star moustache bedraggled, the slim nose puffy. I sense decay. Soon he will be oily and fat.

He came and stood next to me.

He is gorgeous.

"I was in bed twenty minutes ago. Had to get a taxi in…" Salvatore turned abruptly and I was forsaken for the female student friend with a growing-out permanent wave, no makeup, large pink framed spectacles and today she wore a yellow woollen cardigan darned at the elbows. Salvatore marched her, arm in arm, into the corridor to talk, then he returned, ignoring authority – authority being the cadaver and the hideously-hatted woman – and strode over to me. "Why don't you wear jeans like the rest of us?"

"Jeans are your uniform. I don't do uniforms."

"But that?"

I had, on arrival at the office, been the floor show as I took off Victor's garish windcheater to reveal the lightweight sweater which Victor had described as garish with zigzag stripes in pink and deep mauve and strident green on a background of white. There were stars jarring in orange. Madge had cried with laughter. Alice screamed. Hamish took me aside and congratulated me.

"I like to conform," I said to Salvatore.

"Who are you kidding?"

The woman in the hat disappeared and the clerks relaxed and the noise level rose to the usual bedlam.

Salvatore said, "You couldn't give a shit what anyone thinks about you."

"You saying I think I am superior to everyone?"

"Your sneering voice tells me that," he said.

"That is very hurtful."

"Who do you respect?" he said.

"No one in authority."

"You do lust after me?"

"Take a shower then ask. You stink like a donkey's arse."

"So you don't fancy me now?" he said.

"You're unfaithful. You go to coffee with that bitch – the only hot thing about her is her charity shop woolly."

"Do not call her a bitch," he said. "I am not disloyal."

"Bloody right you are if you prefer that spectacle-wearing cow to me."

“You’re outrageous,” he said.

“Tomorrow I shall swap my camp clothes for a hair shirt and will wear old jeans with holes in them. I will be as I am today, protesting, rebelling against unfair authority but you’re so obsessed with ‘whether I fancy you’ that you can’t see it.”

“Yours is an overt declaration of your homosexuality by two-fingering the dictates of authority by wearing those camp clothes,” he said.

“I’ll give you a reluctant eight out of ten. If I wear smart jeans I will be conforming, won’t I?”

“You’ve got my admiration but will those in authority get it? Many are women. Authority in a woman is often frightening – think Thatcher. Think Enid. Enid is a neat worker; the result of early toilet training in childhood. And you’re right. The women here would concentrate on the sex in you. Your hair bleached looks good. You’re hot and up for it like a whore.”

I love talking with him when he accuses me of being a sexy whore.

I said, “I am humbled by your words. I am a devotee on my knees. Please allow me to have coffee with you?”

“Why have you gone girlie? It’s that sweater. Rubbed off camp. Come to coffee with my girlfriend.”

“No! No! No!”

“You sound like Thatcher only less masculine.”

“Don’t you get it? I am jealous of your girlfriend.”

“Can I tell her?” he said.

“Sure.”

“It will make for a stimulating discussion. You being dressed like ageing expensive rent and she a scullery maid. She would choose you sexually.”

“With you around? And ditch the ageing bit.”

"She is attracted to your disdain."

"Tell her I am queer," I said.

"She knows. Makes you more interesting."

Perfect eyebrows and his black hair is so beautiful that I felt privileged to put my arm in his and he accepted it because it would show his student friend he supported my right to be queer.

I said, "Don't worry, I have a new boyfriend, I'm crazy about but to be this close to you has me erect." I clung to his arm as he kept nervously glancing at me.

"Don't you want to see it?" Naomi's manner was unusually sharp. Her sunburn looks so painful it must be classified as a burn.

Glancing at the ring on her finger, I said, "Engaged to…?"

Her face was on fire. "It should be you."

"Talk to me?"

"He's Malaysian, dark and sexy and in for lunch the other day in the restaurant. The prejudice gave me a migraine."

I said, "Get yourself to the sick bay. Come back and I'll take you home in taxi."

"It's not the sunburn, it's the bigots." She had tears running down her cheeks as she left for the sickbay.

Daniel dumped a noisy pile of work next to me then spent time studying my outrageous clothes and hair.

"It's you doing a Hamish?"

"You could say that," I said, enjoying the companionship of Danny.

"You've got Wayland's vote."

"I always have Wayland's vote but not yours?"

Daniel ignored my flirting, so I said, "Heard about your jaunt on Sunday to the beach."

Wayland had earlier told me that they did over a hundred on the cliff road but the car gave up the ghost entering the car park where two young women waved. Wayland was alert, tall, suntanned and as he spends time in the gym he is now a very presentable young man.

Naomi arrived back from the sick bay and sat the other side of Daniel, said to him, "That girl was all over Wayland." Then she said to me, "Did you honestly do it with him?"

"If he says I did, I did."

"Hate you, Ralph. And I *loathe* you, Danny, you're not even red," said Naomi.

"Car buggered, Dan?" I said.

"Ten thousand miles ago. Gave it a push when it cooled down. When it started, it sounded like MasterBates-man without his inhaler. Naomi, your face?"

"The nurse didn't put anything on it without seeing a doctor," she said.

I said, "Nude bathing was it, Danny?"

"With her? You joke." We both examined the suffering Naomi who looked at the waiting nurse from the sick bay and said,

"She's giving me a lift to Outpatients."

When she left, Daniel said, "You a beach-goer, Ralph? The tan? Can't be gardening? Can't see you getting excited over Brussels sprouts?"

"I am the Quentin Crisp of the horticultural world. I do not dust my lilies."

"What's that mean? Sex?"

"Skydiving."

"You jammy bastard. It's turned your hair white."

"You know when you are petrified but there is no way you can go back?"

"This is about you being with a bloke, isn't it? I knew it. You'd risk your life for a fuck."

"He reckons it's better than sex. I was falling and the ground stayed a million miles away and I didn't want the parachute to open."

Daniel stopped smiling. "You wanted to die?"

"The good bit is it got me a proper job in… You know that small airfield south of here? Sort of homely with a grass runway, a windsock and a few wonky huts black with creosote? Good fun. The canteen is Graham's wife and whoever mucks in. They are extending the runway, putting up new buildings, so I'm doing some evenings and all weekends. The flying freebies I'm trying to avoid."

Daniel looked despondent as he said, "This bloke you going with, works there?"

"Yeah, I'm lucky with him."

"You'll be working with him and when looking out the window you'll get to see planes taxiing. And the freebies? Jesus, that is living, Ralph. Knowing you, you'll have sex for lunch – and tea." Daniel's perfect skin was gloriously tanned. His long arm reached out and a large hand flicked through piles of cards ready for the sort machine. "Dead boring here. No one takes it seriously except for…" his voice dropped to a whisper so Enid sitting opposite could not hear, "…Enid."

I said brightly to Enid, "I need a new pencil? Down to a stub. Am I eligible?"

She hurried to the bosses' drawer, took out a pencil and was about to hand it over. "Just a minute." Then she moved briskly to the sharpener fixed to a shelf.

Daniel looked at me. "Sad, innit?"

I have taken the day off and am pretend-sick but I am genuinely ill. It is one of those days when I could not go to the office, but now with Punk away, everyday seems one of those days. I know that this or that pain is psychosomatic, an indication of something wrong with me mentally.

A knock on my front door. Wayland, my carer, had taken the day off too – officially as leave. He is too good to be true, I told him, as he made salad for our lunch and I hammered home my message.

"This is the last time. Us alone, I mean. Punk would not approve," I said.

"I'll pop out and restock your larder in a minute. No milk."

"You never say to me, You're out of milk *again!* Love you for it. Milk or no milk we're seeing too much of each other's underwear. It has to stop. I am serious about Punk and you have this girl."

"Danny calls her a greedy bitch."

"Oh, fuck," I said.

"Can I suck you off before I get your shopping in?"

"No, you cannot. I am ill. And very tired. And loyal."

"You need washing powder. I've made a list. Is Punk up with the shopping stuff? I do all Gran's now," he said.

"I have to be faithful to Punk. And I have to make it work between Punk and me. That may sound phoney but I mean it."

Wayland undid my fly and carefully held my hard. "I'm up for the big casino when I get back. I expect you have lubricant?" He looked me in the eyes and said, "You giggling should be a turn off but it only makes me more eager to be penetrated."

My hands were in his hair, his mouth damp and familiar on my cock and me gasping. I came quickly, always quickly with him.

I said, "You shouldn't have swallowed it. You don't know where I've been."

"It's nice and warm in my tummy and you wouldn't put me at risk."

"You shouldn't trust people. And no to penetration."

"You've stopped hearing those voices, haven't you?"

"I didn't know I'd told you I heard voices? Not often, but scary. And yeah, they've gone."

He rested on the carpet, leaning back between my legs as he scribbled a list. "I'll get some of that ham. Gran really enjoyed it. They sell smashing sausage rolls. Get some. And no more sex. I can see you are serious. Later you can kiss me while I wank. That doesn't count, does it? He sounds your type. Different, I mean. Danny told me to stand back and give you air."

"I'm going to live with someone not emigrating to China."

"It's more than that with this Punk, isn't it?" he said. "I mean, he'll be the one who feels real at home here, like I do?" He bit his lip. "Will you give him Aramis, Ralph?"

The supervisor was panicking that there isn't enough work and his expression is a perpetual moan. Too little or too much work has him charging up and down the office.

"He didn't get satisfaction last night. His wife has her hair done Mondays," said Enid, coming down on the workers' side for a change.

Freddie had his hand on my shoulder and his hand

stayed there when he told me he leaves this weekend for Australia. Freddie is looking anywhere and everywhere for someone to care for him, and he looks more frantically now he is nearing middle age. Why Australia? He never took me up on my offer to try to get him a job at sea. He is the laboratory rat trapped in a cage desperately seeking something. Wayland wasn't. Wayland knew what he wanted and went straight for it. I didn't stand a chance.

Freddie said, "It's for how long…? No idea. If I run out of cash and come back with my tail between my legs after a few months it'll have them saying, Told you so."

My job at the airfield would be up and running in less than two weeks as the new office was nearing completion but I had not given in my notice and trusted only Daniel and Wayland with that information.

Freddie said, "What I want to do is pan for gold."

"You're in orbit."

"Kalgoorlie, kid. And when I am swilling my pans and wearing my hat with corks a-bobbing, I will feel a tap on my shoulder and it will be you."

"Bloody won't. I'll be in the pub and you're paying."

"Thanks for listening to my shit," he said, squeezing my shoulder in a final farewell.

Not a final farewell for on the following Tuesday I saw Freddie outside the Post Office in town talking animatedly to two women from the office.

Earlier, that day's mail had brought three postcards postmarked Australia.

Enid said, "He's well travelled. Twenty thousand miles, two air terminals and three I-have-almost-made-it post-cards. Heathrow and a blanket would have been cheaper."

"He sold his car and everything," said Ginny. "I feel sorry for his friend if she takes him back."

Always his friend never his girlfriend or partner.

Daniel followed me into the cloakroom, his usual cheerful face miserable. "Getting married. Wanted Freddie to be my best man."

"You're okay, he's back."

"Saw him. Won't come to the wedding."

"I can't stand weddings. Maybe he can't? I know he likes you," I said.

Hurt showed in Daniel's eyes. "For what?"

"Come to my place for a bite to eat? Punk, my free-falling live-in boyfriend is home and has forbidden me to approach the stove. Tomas has my cooking on the official poison list. You can drink beer or Château plonk and eat cheese and Ryvita unless… Tomas! Tomas is back being wonderful. He's fixed my guttering. I'll ring him then you'll get to meet two friends of mine. You might like them. One I tried to kill and the other has me jumping out of planes."

"Dunno."

"You do know, you miserable shit. It'll put you off queers for life." We laughed as we raced upstairs to the pay phone. We squeezed into the telephone booth, shut the door. I dialled.

"Tomas, I'm cooking this evening. Break in the new cooker. I thought steak."

His "You are *not* cooking steak!" was so violent that Daniel heard and laughed.

I winked, took a slug out of my hip flask, gave it to Daniel.

Tomas said, "I'll cook."

I said, "You do know I am now vegetarian? I can be

tempted by Danish Blue or a Danish male of any colour. And a young guy from work is coming. He's getting married. You two pathetic heterosexuals can talk wedding plans and get depressed."

"Beef Wellington?"

"Beef Wellington is coming? He can talk to Danish Black." I turned to Daniel, hand over the mouthpiece, said, "I wonder if we can squeeze Wayland in? He is family." That had Daniel grinning and making rude hand movements.

"You still there?" said Tomas.

"Daniel is coming and another chum from work?"

"I'll make you vegetarian pies," said Tomas. "Victor coming?"

"He's got a play to read through. I asked Punk if it was Off Broadway. 'Off High Street,' he said."

"I am assuming Punk will be in attendance?"

"Physically but mentally he's with Proust. He'll be washing up. I bought him a frilly pinny and a bottle of Fairy Liquid. No sense of humour."

"I'll bring him dog food. Five percent chicken, it says on the can."

"Don't you knock him. He can rebuild your car between courses and cut your hair. And his boss wants a male model to promote the airfield? On advertising hoardings throughout the county. I can see you in a leather helmet and goggles and nothing else. Pity about your small cock. Hopefully someone will pencil spectacles over it, make it look like a myopic Hitler."

"I'll do it clothed. Try for a hundred?"

"You'll get thirty."

"So it's me cooking and Punk washing up. You'll have Daniel setting the table. What will you be doing? Flower arranging?" said Tomas.

"I've got to make Wayland feel at home."

"Wayland? You fancy him or something?"

I heard the familiar catch in Tomas' voice and watched a grinning Daniel as I said, "Wayland's straighter than a Roman road. Tomas, do you have a hedge trimmer? Punk was unnecessarily abrupt when I suggested he sharpen the garden shears."

STEPHAN

Fine blue scars stand out on his forehead. At a distance the impression is he's old but close to he's in his twenties. The nose is slightly off and the skin texture on his left cheek isn't as it should be. I've got used to Stephan, got used to him being slow.

In the washroom, he swished water in the hand basin, both taps full on. Stephan, I sensed, was only just in control as he turned off the taps. He removed his spectacles then painstakingly searched for a place to rest them, found a spot on the adjoining sink then he reached for his other spectacles. It took several minutes.

Stephan isn't potty, he has brain damage which affects his reactions, but Stephan is still in there, trouble is most of the time the signals do not get through as quickly as they should.

I was at the urinal – timing him, I suppose.

"How's Ralph?" he said.

"It's getting better but I don't look forward to going to bed alone." I pulled out my hip flask, wiped the top, handed it over.

After a swig, he said, "I'm not good."

I crossed to the sink, stood alongside him. He tugged a

harsh blue paper towel from the wall holder and laboriously dried his hands.

I said, “When you off on holiday?”

His face impassive but in his eyes I could see he was searching for information, going through files. “…July.”

“Where to?” I tried not to be patronising, but both Stephan and I know he is simply not as he should be.

“Cornwall… Falmouth.”

“Rain’s stopped. Fingers crossed.”

“Yeah, yeah, yeah.” Then he saw I was holding open the door for him. “Thank you, Ralph.”

Back in the office he was immersed in his thoughts as he walked in his deliberate way to his desk. Must have leg damage too. The blazer was too large. I expect he shrunk a bit after the explosion. His ability to communicate has been damaged by a mine in the Falklands. Ironic ’cos I probably saw him amongst the wounded when they were ferried on board the hospital ship. Could have chatted to him. Talked to some who were damaged. Some too damaged to be shown on television, a deeply moved cameraman told me when he filmed the casualties. Then he told me that the tapes took two to three weeks to get home. Carrier pigeon would be quicker. ‘Censorship by delay,’ he had said.

On board ship hospitalised were injured Argentinians too. Some conscripts, all deep-down scared and scarred, all eventually had been transferred to an Argentinian hospital ship except for one. My sinecure had been gleaning information from ‘the enemy’. Jesus, the enemy? I was in my twenties and was in loco parentis to one Argentinian child. He looked sixteen. I wrote home for him, telling Mum in Buenos Aires that her son couldn’t write but the marvellous news was the surgeon had saved the sight of one eye and her son was keeping his fingers crossed – if he had had hands – for the sight in the other. Now I wished I had cuddled him but that might have been misinterpreted. Alone and scared; his mates gone, his delicate eye and the surgeon's expertise had him waiting as he was cared for by nurses and was subjected to good natured banter from the injured British squaddies. Always a joke with the Argie as they hand-fed the boy chocolate. Nowadays I can't talk about the wounded to anyone. Can't talk without crying, I mean.

Stephan interrupted my thoughts. "Heard about Freddie."

"He's not coming back to work."

"Nice man. Real sorry for him."

Stephan understood.

THE PEBBLE INN

He is a short man who wears Bakelite bicycle clips and he has on a green beret but not a commando green beret. He sure is stalwart though. Age-wise he could be anything from twenty-five to forty-five. He cleans the local public lavatories. A zealot. The lavatories would win awards. At times he seems to stand guard, waiting for vandals. I find his dedication moving.

I stopped off at the park urinal and had a chat with him. I find the place shuddery now: the flushing urinal, the chill dampness, the walls which he has spray-painted or scrubbed to cover graffiti, but he is warming with conversation and laughter and his love of soccer.

Foggy, and with the forecast of heavy rain brooding, I did not want to go too far and headed for *The Pebble Inn* where the décor is modern-nasty with faux leather banquettes and Artex walls done out in coffee and cream paint. Hopefully it would be almost empty then I could gaze into the mist that shrouds the sea and hear the moaning mournful siren at the end of the breakwater.

The Pebble Inn was packed. Hate crowds but the rain was hitting monsoon intensity, bouncing off the pavement so I ran in to shelter.

The landlady said, “You’re not too wet, my darling?”

I said, “An umbrella. I put it in the plastic bowl in the porch. Wasn’t sure if it was for umbrellas or for dogs?”

“It’s for dog’s umbrellas,” she said, carefully drawing a pint of Guinness without asking me what I wanted. It is this familiarity and being wanted that draws me to the place.

The lack of heat doesn’t draw me. I sat on a chilled banquette nursing my chilled Guinness. Thick black mould coats the sill of the high window. Outside, beyond the narrow road, is a line of shingle and the sea is grey and is pounded flat by torrential rain.

I am writing in my notebook but a loud customer is intruding.

“Young man!” the customer bawled across the lounge to a taxi driver not much younger than himself. “I shall be five minutes. Wait!”

“No chance, mate, double yellow,” said the taxi driver.

“Then drive round the fucking block.”

The taxi driver left.

Talking to Stephan yesterday made me feel bad again. We should avoid the other, avoid the familiarity that triggers memory. I sipped some Guinness and was only able to swallow when I closed my eyes. And when I swallowed there was panic, a desire to grab my notebook and get the hell out into the pelting rain, into the park, to be with the greedy pigeons doing their wet mating display on that shortcut path of mud and grass, and to seek the lavatory to give my message of farewell to the bog cleaner.

"Where's that fucking taxi driver? Fucking phone him!" yelled the man at the landlady.

Being ill makes me aggressive. I am tall. I am the quiet guard dog. I do not bark a great deal but go straight for the jugular.

I stood, said to the objectionable man, "Get out."

"You want a fucking punch, fuck-face?"

Four burly lifeboatmen stood like bodyguards, two either side of me, facing the bully. The man left. I sat. Unfortunately the looks of approval were on me. Unfortunately Vera knows I have been trained in unarmed combat, but the concept of me slamming the moron to the floor had me smiling at her because I was taught to fight dirty, to fight to disable and to win. A free pint of cold Guinness was placed in front of cold me. Now my staying in the pub was my test. I had to down the Guinness so I put a tranquilliser under my tongue because I have read somewhere that that speeds up the rate at which the drug enters the bloodstream. I swallowed a second tablet as a back up. I need different medication for although the voices have gone, the nightmares are still kicking in regularly, I suggested a change of medication to the quacking quack who told me he couldn't do my job and I couldn't do his.

Cunt.

Why bother with the tablets at all? But as a hypochondriac, who is mentally ill, I wonder what I would be like if I didn't take them at all?

I concentrated reading Conrad. He made me forget

about wanting to vomit. Conrad, not the tranquillisers, had done that job. Now I could get down to my headache and swallow the three aspirins with my free pint of Guinness. The glass drained, and the residue of foam lay like brown spume on an industrial foreshore.

The landlady said to a customer, "Are you forty-six, dear?"

The meals are numbered with raffle tickets. The man with clay on the cuffs of his working denims searched for his numbered ticket.

I heard the landlady say, "I should have remembered you were the extra sausage, darling, but what with that horrible man..." She placed another pint of Guinness in front of me, patted my shoulder. I smiled my thanks, watching it settle.

My nerves were steadied. Sure as hell it wasn't the tablets, maybe it was the alcohol or the warm feeling the landlady gave me that did the trick as she put her arm about me.

"Ralph?"

"I look bad?"

"A bit tired."

She turned to her husband who had arrived laden with packages, said, "You missed a gem. Next time I go to cash'n'carry." She turned to me. "Sid thinks you and I are having an affair."

I held her hand.

"What's up, Ralph?" said Sid.

"I've about left the office and am settling down with a bloke. Got a permanent job at the airfield."

"That's good, isn't it?"

"Yeah, I can't sleep and miss him like hell when he is away. Suppose I do like him a lot."

"Another living doll?" said Vera.

"Inside he is. What Plié and he have in common is wanting to get me to jump out of planes. I can't jump."

"You jumped the other Sunday?" said Sid.

"Sid, it is the ongoing commitment that intimidates," said Vera. "Ralph, can you imagine Sid jumping out a plane? With that belly."

"Yes, I can. He's my ultimate. I'd take him on – jumping in tandem, thinking of the sex afterwards," I said to a grinning Sid.

"If you're *that* desperate then there's a job here – evenings?" said Vera.

"I am rude to customers and it would compromise your marriage."

"Ideal," she said. "But I am interpreting what you said as meaning you are committed to the airfield and the new boyfriend but you still feel bad?"

As I nodded, Sid said, as he held a glass under an optic, "I am driven to it."

"The doctor said I have to snap out of it and stop being sorry for myself and work harder," I said.

"I've told you and told you about that man. You've seen Dorothy? Enough said," said Vera. "Get another doctor?"

"I've made an appointment with the new surgery. I am now aiming for a tranquil life."

By jumping out of planes, I thought.

STEPHAN

I watched the supervisor examining a letter as Stephan stood waiting. Today his too-large clothes seemed to fit. He looked more square, more of the man he had been in the military. With him I am completely unshy, something in me alters. I go out of my way to say hello. Suppose it's because we have both watched men die.

His "Hello, Ralph" was instant and there was no dragged out pause when he said, "Hear you're leaving today?" Then he talked frankly about how he was lucky to work here. I asked him if he liked it?

"What else is there for me to do?" he said.

He held the door open for me and as it swung closed behind us, he shook my hand. "Got the rest of the day off. Our reunion. Get pissed. All the best, Ralph."

I was smiling because I think that this is maybe only the third time I've seen him alive and fully communicating. It's in his eyes.

It is this reaction I hope for when I talk with him.

PART THREE – REMEMBRANCE DAY

The downpour suited my sad afternoon. Me handing round chocolate bars and avoiding saying goodbye to too many people. A Marks and Spencer's voucher and a card in my pocket as I hurried down the drive but I got real happy seeing Punk at the wheel of my car. Wayland on the back seat had me wondering.

"Found him dripping in the rain. His girlfriend wants them engaged before sex," said Punk.

"No way. You've only known her for days and Daniel said…" I was still lecturing him as we ran through the rain from the car to my front door.

Slumped in chairs, Punk said, "You two have frozen

chips and the quiche. I'm off seeing Mum. Ralph, easy on the booze. Keep a clear head for tomorrow. You're helping instruct."

"Are you out of your skull? My duties are clerical."

"Instructing gets you proper money and you did instructing last three weekends and Graham and Jasper are impressed."

"Jumping in waders? You seen it?"

"Check your seaweed. Forecast is brilliant," said Punk.

"I'm not a qualified instructor-person and I am a height phobic-person and I shall get paralytic."

"Tomas found you a pain in the ass? Can't understand why. Are you and Wayland staining the sheets?"

"Now you insult my integrity," I said.

Punk said, "Wayland's gran died. He's choked up bad. It's like him losing his mum twice over. He gets the lot: the house and a load of shares and stuff. Wants to ask you about solicitors?"

"Let me go through the paperwork."

Punk said, "Him on his tod is him lost. He won't ask but he wants to stay with us for a bit?"

"I'll pay anything," said Wayland miserably.

I called him over and he sat on his heels on the carpet, his tears and the rain from his hair dampened my jeans. I took his head in my hands and his hair was coarse and wet but I let my hands linger in it then gently holding him, I kissed his eyes, said, "You understand it's me with Punk now if you stay?"

He nodded.

My cheek was tight to his and my hand was on the back of his warm neck as I said, "Go get us tea? Strong."

He left Punk and me.

Punk's oil engrained fingers showed broken nails but

his touch on my hand was as sensitive as a surgeon's. "I saw the pain in his face and the love in yours and I know why I live with you. But I am stopping in otherwise it'll be more than quiche you two are having for supper."

"We drive him home and pick up the paperwork and his clobber and he can stay here but for how long?" I said.

"See how it goes. He needs the stability of a normal home."

I looked at Punk, waiting for the follow up smart remark. None came. When Wayland brought in three mugs of tea, Punk said, "How far is this place of yours?"

"Landrose? The Drive?" said Wayland.

"Bloody hell! Each property in an acre of land. Your girlfriend seen it?"

"She was going through Gran's stuff. Tried on a necklace, wouldn't give it back. Danny told her to hand it over or he'd smack her. Danny came with me and put the jewellery in the bank." Wayland looked scared.

Punk said, "Forget her. You marry and she legally gets half the house. I'll have Mum over for supper and commonsense. She'll talk to you about your Gran's clothes and stuff but you and Ralph cuddling up cosy is not on the cards, not seeing the way you two are. I thought you were any guy off the street, but just now with your hair thick and wet and them sexy ears and..." Punk thought, said, "You two together had me in tears."

I said, "Tomorrow?"

"Get stuck in with Jasper. He's got fifteen for first day instruction, seven women."

"No jumping then?"

"Didn't say that."

"Isn't that what first day instruction means?"

"Wayland and me will have the quiche. You've them

cheese-less pies to finish," said Punk.

"No way. Tomas must loathe me. Think potato and pastry heavy as lead."

"HP sauce should do the trick."

I started to giggle.

"What?" he said. "HP sauce is the best."

"We have your mum over tomorrow. Who is cooking?"

"She is."

"Punk, for Christ's sakes! I'll get a Chinese."

"She won't eat Oriental."

"I'll buy a steak pie and a trifle?"

Wayland said, "I'll cook? Last year I froze black-currants and the beans and carrots I grew. You want I check Gran's freezers, get stuff over?"

"You cook and do gardens? I am thinking hedges?" said Punk.

"Take me a day?"

"You're the man," said Punk, then to me, "Tomorrow I'm scheduling you freefalling with a fit guy off the cover of a fag mag – no shit. I fancy his car. He fancies you. I take his Aston Martin for a spin. You take him in the staff room. Twenty minutes and two condoms should do it."

"Can I say, fuck off?"

"Give it a whirl. And don't give me that horse manure about you being faithful, Ralph. Your second name is, I want to shag the fag mag hunk."

"You can trust Ralph," said Wayland.

"Ten minutes out of my sight and I hose him down in the yard. Ralph, is he a yes or a no?" A magazine cover was unfolded in front of my eyes.

"Jesus Christ, make it two condoms and a bottle of Moet Chandon. Rain's stopped. Let's get the food convoy on the road."

As we walked to the car, Wayland said to me, "You're not really two-timing Punk?"

Punk said to me, "Well?"

"No hanky panky, I promise. I would never betray your trust in me."

"Sarcasm means, he is," said Punk, starting the engine.

I said, "Wayland, tomorrow is Saturday. I want you at the airfield in Levis, no underwear. Loose-button your fly. I want glimpses of young pubic hair."

Punk said to me, as we drove towards Wayland's house, "Seven women. I'll cut his hair. The quiff goes, so does his virginity."

"Slim, tanned young body. I'll have him on display in a harness. The women will salivate."

Wayland said, "How about Dover sole and apple pie tomorrow? A mushroom omelette for Ralph?"

"I'll help you. Ralph will be doing the accounts," said Punk, "This fag mag hunk, Ralph? You giving him a seeing to?"

"After our jump, I suppose I could…"

"You can't!" said Wayland from the back seat. Hearing the pain in his voice I understood how deeply he was grieving.

"Why can't I?" I turned to face him.

"Because you can't," he said, his voice shaky.

Punk said to Wayland, "With you as his talking chastity belt, he won't."

"But…" said Wayland.

"We're joking. He wouldn't do that to me 'cos it would break my heart," said Punk.

"His quiff stays but blond?" I said, deeply moved by Punk's declaration and now uncomfortably obligated.

"And the fag mag guy?" said Punk.

"I do not want to jump!"

"You'd jump with Wayland?" said Punk, his hand briefly on my knee.

I knew what he was up to. He had to wean Wayland off me and hopefully onto girls on the course. Also he was obligating me to jump again.

"Wayland, you are about to become a skydiving man," said Punk.

"Don't know."

Punk said, "A few days compassionate leave next week is you doing the course."

Wayland said nothing.

"You've got to pay Graham. I'll negotiate him down but it won't come cheap."

In Wayland's home, Punk said, "I am looking at oil paintings and chandeliers."

Wayland said, "You want I collect a vacuum cleaner?"

"Ralph's got one someplace." Punk looking about him, said, "You own this and you want to stay with us?"

"Lonely. Nights are bad."

Punk nodded at me. "He knows about loneliness at night. Women and blokes break ankles running after him but when he's asleep, he is plagued by bad dreams and wakes up alone but when I hold him he knows he is okay. So he puts up with me making him jump out of planes. Wayland, go make a lightning raid on your food store."

"I'll start on the freezer in the utility room," said Wayland sounding as though he was staying with us for the duration.

After he left, Punk slid open doors at the far end of the hall. "Wayland is loaded. He needs shielding against the piranhas." We were looking at a good sized indoor pool. The opposite wall was seemingly all glass; the view was of a darkening sea and the harbour mouth where a turquoise flashing light marked the end of the breakwater. Punk said, "You water the plants, I'll check the pump."

I had finished plant watering and Punk was taking off his jeans for a swim when Wayland appeared.

"Food and the chainsaw for the hedges are in the car."

Punk studied him. "You've got it. The snug t-shirt. And the way your jeans sit on your hips. Hands above your head and breathe in." Punk turned to me. "As a lecher, how does he grab you?"

"He's wank material. The smooth skin and glimpses of navel and underarm hair… The face broods."

"Okay for me to swim?" said Punk.

Wayland said, "Anything you want."

Punk said softly to him, "You and Ralph? Anything?"

"Never like that."

"Tell me how you feel for Ralph?"

"With him when my hands are sweating, he holds them, never says nothing but he holds on. He doesn't mind who sees us. Him and me talk stuff I can't talk about to no one else."

"He said you prefer women?" said Punk.

"I'd do anything for him," said Wayland. "He told me never to tell anyone what we did 'cos what we did was private between us. But when he told me I could tell you, I got sad, knew it was over. I can't jump, Punk."

"Your back?" I said.

"I'm a loser," said Wayland, biting his lower lip.

"Bollocks, a fit bloke like you? Once you get a taste for it…"

I said, "Punk, how about that swim? Let me talk to

him?"

Punk looked hurt as he stripped off. Wayland was mesmerised by Punk's physique as he dived, making barely a ripple. We sank into deep cushions, opening cans of Coke, watching him cutting through the water.

Wayland said, "Tomorrow?"

"In the forces I had to pass a swimming test. Fully clothed, wearing shoes. After two lengths, I had to tread water for three minutes. Went to pull myself out the pool. The sergeant put his foot on my hands. I was then treading water for another three minutes. Gasping for air. Hands on the pool's edge. Hands got trod on again."

"You saying what? That I can jump?"

"Tomorrow come up in the plane? Jump harnessed to me? I've been where you are now."

Punk, resting at the far end of the pool, was watching us, his muscular legs floating, his soft sex surrounded by dark hair. He wanted me to persuade Wayland to jump; nothing to do with Wayland joining the chest-thumping brigade of men; this was about him losing his naiveté that had him dishing out jewellery to girls on the make. And getting him relating to the women on the course.

I watched the sun set over a dusk-grey sea; small box-like rectangles of ships were silhouetted on the horizon, the red sky was layered with ominous clouds.

"Seeing you with Punk is good," said Wayland, not jealous only wanting me to be happy.

"He's real sensitive but has a blind spot when it comes to leaping out of planes."

Alone with me and now at ease, Wayland said, "The guy with the Aston Martin?"

"He'll jump with Punk."

"If I can't jump? I'll still pay. Gran left me a shedload

of cash," he said.

"Never tell anyone that you are loaded. And if you don't want to jump, you don't. I'll talk it over with Graham."

He nodded.

I said, "You'll jump 'cos I know how you feel."

"Feel about you?" he said.

"Some of that is there. But this is your big chance. Grab it. It'll enrich your life. Sounds phoney but it's true. In the plane tomorrow, it's adrenaline time. The engine racket. The wind noise. The excitement…"

"We are harnessed together?"

"Sure."

Wayland would jump. In the plane is being ready to jump.

"About your first jump, Ralph? Tell me?"

"No!" I could hear my voice breaking.

"Why're you so upset?"

"Nothing."

"Tell me?" he said.

I shook my head.

"Ralph?"

Could I tell him of a life so different? The course I did when I trained with the lads from the Parachute Regiment? The two mavericks were me and Plié. Plié didn't whinge like I did but we bonded because despite me being terrified of jumping, I was a marine, and however crap a marine I was, Plié had to stand by me 'cos he followed the marines' ethos of team spirit, cheerfulness in adversity, humility and determination. 'You okay?' he'd say then he would groan at my, 'I am not going to jump.' He said,

'You're not weaselling out, Gobshite.' When I strained a muscle, that had him worrying that I would miss the course. A course I could not complete without him, he told me with no humility. So I had to be massaged. Embrocation on my lower back which was kneaded by the dishy Plié. When he finished I told him I couldn't stand up because I had a hard on. 'You would with me massaging you,' he said, his humility showing again, 'Two more minutes and I'll have had you shooting your load.' I said, 'You must massage me daily. I can't make it with my bad back.' He said, 'Cheerfulness, Ralph? I don't hear cheerfulness in adversity? All I hear is you bellyaching all the fucking time. You'll fucking jump or I'll smash your fucking face in.' That was his commando sensitivity kicking in. I said, 'Your job is to look after me. Problem is the paras are better than me.' That went home 'cos no one is better than a marine. He said, 'You hear yourself? It's not better than *me*, it's better than *I*. And you went to a Grammar School? Sorry, I forgot, you're a Ruskie.' I said, 'My mother is Russian and I hate her.' He was open mouthed as he asked why? I said, 'Because she brought me into this cruel world where I am alone and being bullied by a brute.' His face softened with a grin. 'You've got brutish me to look after you now, not mummy. It was a girl's school you went to, wasn't it?' I said, 'The Kirov.' When he said, 'Plié?' we were so much in sync. I said, 'You've done ballet?' He said, 'Piss off. My sister tried to get me to do the pas de deux.' I said, 'And you would do it 'cos you're an arrogant shit who has to show her how wonderful you are.' Plié decided he would call me Sergei. He said Sergei with a lisp. That's commando humour with only him laughing. I said if he did, I would call him Diaghilev. His dark blue eyes narrowed. 'Queer, wasn't he?' I said, 'He was a cunt of a task master with looks to get me hard.' I wasn't called Sergei but he massaged my lower back daily. A massage so sublime I reckon my mattress gave birth later. He had accepted me, so I continued with the course, trying my damnedest. How I tried for him. Man-stuff for Plié. Marines are stomach churning, they stand up for each other. They are unselfish and hard to hate – well, most are and it has to be on a good day with the wind in the right direction.

The day before my first jump I got into a funk. I ditched ethos and Plié, and went straight to the instructor to tell him I was refusing to jump. Rules were crystal clear, I would be returned to unit immediately and would never be accepted on a course again. Rules that did not apply to me it appeared. The instructor wanted to know why I was giving up when I had done all the hairy scary bits in the hard slog of preliminary training when three others had chickened out at the tower. The fact was I had got through training because Plié was as sexy as hell and swore at me most of the time. The instructor said he would 'like it' if I go up in the plane at the end of the line to get used to the plane. And he solemnly promised I would not jump.

Being in the plane means being ready to jump.

Seeing the aircraft next day had my bowels jelly. A menacing dark beast, gigantic with four massive engines. The months of basic training and the commando training had been to condition me to obey orders without question. We were mustered and inspected. We boarded. All men bulky with parachutes. All men silent. Orderly. The plane was speeding along a runway streaked black with rubber. The monster was airborne. No going back. Engine noise. Lined up, clipped on, tensed up. Close together.

Concentrating on any hand signals. Ready for the first jump. Plié was heading the column. Door open. Wind racket. Plié looking out, looking down, like he was running the show; then looking back for me. Saw me. Nodded. The light was green. First out was Plié. Drilled and smooth, the men followed, almost doubling. Go, go, go… static-line jumping has to be fast to concentrate the troops in the drop zone.

The instructor had lied. I wasn't the last. The instructor was last. And a glance at the seen-it-all-before dispatcher, menacing at the gateway to a vertigo hell, told me he would push me out.

Being in the plane means being ready to jump.

At the celebratory piss up a week later with eight jumps under my belt and wings sewn on my uniform, Plié said, 'Good effort, Ralph. We are seconded. We are now in Intelligence.' Half cut, I told the instructor that I had had to buy new underwear each day to get through the course. His response was to whisper to Plié who then went to the heads. When Plié returned, he pushed his folded underpants in my pocket. Plié and the instructor were in hysterics but, cocky with drink, I told smug Plié I'd console myself in them that night. The instructor told me to save my energy because the next day was the start of advanced training for the both of us. 'If any of the paras have thoughts about marines not being the best this is you sticking up two fingers.'

The idea of me in Intelligence was even more absurd than me jumping from a plane. But the fact was I was born in Russia and I had jumped from a plane. My linguistic ability made me exceptional, the instructor told me. Plié echoed, 'You're *numero uno,* Ralph. I'm to look after you, seeing you're totally fucking useless.' Then, 'You're not getting mortal tonight.' So he finished my pint, adding, 'The things I do for my country. Buy me another pint.' This was the sarcastic bastard's way of looking after me with one hand in my wallet and the other hand on my shoulder. He added, 'And a nice massage for Ralph if he's a good boy.'

Punk was watching keenly from the other end of the pool. I could never tell Punk my story but I told Wayland.

When I had finished, Wayland said, "You've still got his underpants?"

"How did you know?"

"Ralph, I can't bear to see you crying."

"You got any booze? Four fingers should do it."

After parachute training Plié and I worked together. The real important time was in the Lebanon where we trained in the Israeli controlled area. Plié and I kept fit with early starts – running before the sun got too hot. We worked under a blond guy who was ace but Plié's illogical certainty had him classified as 'a bender'. My logicality had me asking him why I had to jump out of planes, run until my lungs packed up for Intelligence work? The blond guy said, 'To see if you are suitable for the job.' But I had already failed by refusing to jump. He'd know that but Intelligence took the risk because I was 'Russian' and a linguist. I was put through several silly tests which culminated in an Italian psychiatrist asking stupid questions so I gave stupid answers. His conclusion was Plié was reliable but I was devious and dangerous and a probable killer – so I read in his notes. One thing he got right was I am devious. I can read Italian upside down.

Plié remained in the Lebanon while I flew to

Vladivostok to be Russian again. There I was detained for hours whilst immigration rang Moscow who looked up files and contacted my mother in Leningrad. Everything about me was British but when I opened my mouth I was Russian. I wanted to travel through the country so I caught the trans-Siberian to Moscow where I bought Russian clothes right down to my underwear then on to Leningrad where my mother dragged me round the Winter Palace, so ornate, so opulent with its works of art and its thousands of rooms and stairways dripping ormolu. And there she told me that I looked so happy that I must have found a man? I showed her Plié's photograph and she said, 'You take after your mother, you have good taste.'

Back in Lebanon the blond guy taught us observation, and how to fight dirty, and briefed us over and over about our target. On the sixth week Plié declared, 'The pressure is on, Ralph. This is the big one. He's in town.' On a sweltering morning we caught a bus with Plié sitting well behind me, watching out for me as I cosied up to a man who looked like he'd kill for tuppence. His thigh was pressing urgently in response to mine. I could see his hard bucking his cheap cotton slacks. He was the Syrian for sure, randy and he spoke bad French, had bad breath and teeth pleading for a dentist. Told him my hotel was too risky. Black hairs were thick on the backs of his hands. A hairy hand was on my bare knee then near heading up the leg of my shorts. My own hand briefly brushed the head of the cock of a man who had a history of blowing up people. Notch 'em up, I thought. And if that didn't get me flaccid nothing would. Got off. Watched the bus in the reflection of a shop window. He had followed. We spoke in Russian, and I spoke of my love for that country. We got on. We held hands surrounded by bomb damage. Well, it wasn't

Eastbourne. It wasn't love. It was me psyching up the bastard for sex. My endearments hit pay dirt as he said I would buy a bottle of vodka for myself and cigarettes for this old romantic so we could enjoy a chat and a smoke afterwards. A careful counting of notes. Notes placed tenderly in my hand before he disappeared through a gated archway.

My heart was about to explode with excitement and anticipation when Plié was alongside me. Plié was supposed to keep out of sight as backup. I said, 'He thinks I am a Russian from a delegation to Syria who has taken time out to nose around Lebanon so he trusts me. He was going to share information. But if he has seen me with you I could be in Queer Street.' Plié said, 'You're in that, Ralph. And you ain't whoring with no terrorist.' Plié had deliberately cocked up. If he hadn't, I would have had to have sex with a praying mantis of a man. Awesomely erotic maybe, but dying after coitus was not in my job description but with Plié looking after me, it gave me the opt out clause. Plié had the radio, so I said, 'Press the let's-get-the-hell-out-of-here button.' Sending our location gave us a minimum of five minutes before the cavalry arrived. I led Plié to the arch under which the Syrian had disappeared. The gate was open. From the street-side of the arch, I could hear men's voices loud and happy in a courtyard. Plié suggested looking for a rear way in. I said, 'No time. Report a probable three other men, speaking Arabic. Not local. Alcohol.' Plié was talking into a shielded mouthpiece, firming his earpiece to hear better. Not discreet. Worrying. Pedestrians looking. He whispered, 'We are to kill them all.' Taking his ear-piece and listening in, I said to Plié, 'Tell him to Say again?' The 'Kill all men.' was repeated in my ear. Plié said to me,

‘How old are they?’ I said, ‘They sound students and their talk is of soccer and sex and films.’ He said, ‘I’m not a happy bunny, Ralph? Take them prisoner?’ Very dicey, I thought, two of us against four men at least. If it was a hideout it was almost certain there would be others in the house. But there was no time to debate nor moralise for soon the Syrian would be looking for his vodka pal and there would be the squeal of brakes from our transport. And importantly our target would disappear, having identified me. Our orders were to kill. Plié on the radio, had me putting my Browning in his hand, unzipping his holdall and taking out his Sten. When Plié whispered that backup would be with us in under two minutes, I cocked the Sten and sped under the arch.

Rocking glasses slopped beer on a round-top table. Rolling bottles spilled beer as three panicking dark-skinned young men, sexy in tight European fashion clothes, kicked chairs out the way; frantic to escape. They didn’t. The Sten was accurate but predictable. It jammed on bullet four. My mistake was to leave the dreamboat from the bus till last. The dreamboat was aiming an AK-47 as Plié winged him. I was banging the Sten on the paving stones to clear it. Then I aimed at the man’s chest and pressed the trigger.

I woke in a nursing home with a searing pain in my side which had me asking the motherly nurse if she could hold my hand while I screamed. She gave me morphine. Gave me her hand too. And as Plié opened wide the doors onto a balcony, she told me that he had been with me for three days, washing me and only leaving to go to the lavatory. When my heart had stopped, he broke down and wept. I got emotional and said, ‘I love him.’ She said, kissing Plié’s cheek as she left the room, ‘You are a lovely couple.' French was not Plié's strong point so he said to me, oozing humility, 'Works every time. They can't hold it in. She sees me and has to change her knickers.' I tried to enlighten him but I was talking to the view of a blue Mediterranean and a cluster of romantic palm trees and Plié snoring. He woke four hours later to tell me I must claim compensation from VQ69. I asked, 'Who?' He said, 'Our blond hermaphrodite mincing in Mesopotamia. Told the Vaseline Queen you took a bullet because the Sten is a museum piece and has a history of jamming. Never blame your weapon, he told me. Who is this man? Don't think he's Israeli, they don't need our help? Your Browning fires way to the left for me but it got that mad fucker off balance that's why you only caught a ricochet. Ralph will be compensated.' Plié added, 'I am to give that joker your report soon as you regain consciousness.' I said, 'My right foot, Plié? Pins and needles?' He said, with his fingers playing with my toes, 'I reckon you'll get a stack of cash. Can I have half?' I said, 'No way. Seeing how property prices are rising, I am going to buy a house.' He said, 'Can I have half?' I said, 'No, you fucking cannot.' He said, 'I want you to remember the commando ethos instilled into us during training, Ralph? Courage, cheerfulness in the face of adversity and unselfishness?' I said, 'I am to give you half a house?' He said, 'I'll do the other foot while you think about it.' He fell asleep cuddling my feet to the smile of the nurse when she brought in a tray. He woke, saw compassion in her eyes as she patted his hand. He said, after she left the room, 'Have I fucking got it or not?' When I asked him for a bedpan, he said, 'I've done your feet. Now it's your arse.' He was so manly, he should have been on recruiting posters. A square jaw in a square face. Muscular sexy suntanned arms lifted me. He said, 'That stinks.' When he returned from the sluice room, his eyes were closing from tiredness. I said, 'You've the longest eyelashes ever.' He said, 'I know.' I said, 'Plié?' He said, 'You want a slash?' I said, 'You were right.' He said, 'I was wrong. The three smooth dudes were on the shoot-on-sight list, VQ69 told me.' I said, 'That's horse shit. I heard them talk. They were hard up students out for free beer and a laugh. The guy without the shirt? The chest to die for? I got him in the heart.' Plié said, 'Deadly shooting with that relic from the Imperial War Museum.' I said, 'The short guy, cute with the wild hair? He was pleading as he fell to his knees. Praying to the killer with a gun. What the hell am I?' Plié said, 'Hello, Ralph? This is a war? They were quaffing ales with a terrorist who was nursing an AK-47. Queer Man U fans maybe but they were killers. You followed orders. That was an execution. Your sword was bloodied but your conscience is clear. They picked the right man as leader, Ralph.' I said, 'Tell him I want big money. The psychiatrist put in my report that I was a killer. I must be, mustn't I?' Plié took my cock and put it in the bottle, said, 'It shrank with fear when it saw the priest but I let him stay 'cos he meant well. You naked, looking good, your body, the tan, the stitches and that – dead you looked good. I was thinking necrophilia. Took a photo in case you didn't make it. I'll have it framed for the mantelpiece of our new house. Ten medicos. Machines. Needles. Standing back. Did you hear me shout, Ralph? They went for it for a second time. Fucking zilch! Jesus, Ralph, I thought you'd left me. Their faces solemn. They could have been shaking their heads. I screamed at them *Fucking do it again!* Always the lazy bastard you – taking your time.' It was humbling to see such a man kneeling by my bedside. I said, 'Always do what you want, don't I?' He said, 'You not had that piss? I'll turn on a tap.'

The compensation almost paid for half of our house where I convalesced with Plié for four months. After that our reputation got us calling the shots and insisting on more 'sensitive' postings. Mostly embassy work. We were the boys! Two dashing soldiers who charmed foreign delegates at receptions. Muscular Plié with smooth skin and cheekbones so arrogant and eyes so blue, he riveted the gaze. We got the drinks, eavesdropped and smooth-talked; Plié dazzled the ladies and we socialised with the visiting diplomats' staff over meals. VQ69 had taught us well. Charisma, careful chat and a few bottles of wine yielded a surprising fund of information. But best were our nights off. Him and me in our room. Heaven was a case of beers, Johnny Cash and getting mellow.

Wayland had been talking to Punk and seeing me watching, Wayland hurried over. The large tumbler of scotch, put in my hand, rattled ice. "I told Gran ages ago how you were kind to me. She said I was to buy you a drink. I didn't 'cos I was too shy to ask you."

"Shy? You seduced me." I sipped my drink. Wayland sat on his heels, waiting for me to finish my story:

"After four years together Plié went back to the marines to do 'a man's job' and 'the marines need me in this Falklands War, Ralph.' Because I was *numero uno* Plié got me an appointment in a hospital ship which is safe from attack under the Geneva Convention. Life was empty without him. The South Atlantic depressing. Early afternoon the Tannoy ordered me to an incoming helicopter. The ship at anchor, the sea choppy and grey, the sky sullen as I crouch-ran to the Royal Navy WASP noisy on the helideck.

"Knew it was him, soon as I saw him, even with his face covered. On a stretcher, one arm showing. The drip still in. Read his dog tag. His name and number. Twenty-seven years old and the bastard had left me. The medic said Plié's last request had been to see Ralph. But with the ship in sight he had shouted 'Sergei!' and died. I went to lift the lint that covered Plié's face to look at him for a last time but the medic held my wrist, shook his head. Plié would want that. He was such a conceited bastard."

"You'd say a pray like I did for Gran?" said Wayland.

"Plié and me don't do prayers. I held his hand, knelt, rested my head on his body until the medic said, 'We're calling time, Ralph. Going back to the Cote D'Azure. Him too. The marines look after their own.' I said, 'Got room for one more? I'll clean him.' He said, 'Others will… You do know…?' I finished it for him, '…know that the muscles go in death. Returning a favour. I'll do his interpreting? I speak better Spanish. Even a burro speaks Spanish better than he does.' The medic said, 'Sure ain't the Ritz ashore but the lads are okay.' He was shouting in my ear above the engine racket, 'You've got to inform the ship that you're coming with us before we lift off. A hospital ship's neutral status has them neurotic about radio contact with the shore and the Argies will use any excuse.'

"With my am round Kenny, a stretcher-bearer, I told him that I was going ashore maybe for good. I'd send for my gear. And as we rose in the air, I looked down at the helideck, at Kenny with his arm raised in a farewell salute, at the lines ready in case they had to use foam, at the fire-fighting party about to stand down. I was going to do Plié's job, I wondered? I could wear his gear but I was not fit. Although the medic knew my name I was in a mess-room boiler-suit with no badge of rank or unit and no beret, so I gave him my paybook, saying, 'I used to be an apology for a bootneck.' He said, 'You ain't no apology, Ralph. We all know you. You're the pinup. Plié showed us The Photo of you naked and – dead. On and on he goes how Ralph speaks Russian backwards and how Ralph is brilliant at Arabic and how single-handed Ralph wiped out four terrorists singing *What a Friend We Have in Jesus.* How Ralph took a bullet for him. Ralph got himself a medal, got pissed and wept for the dead as he slung it in the oggin.' I said, 'Plié's shit. I got wounded, got useless. He was the action man. Same like now – him on active service getting dead and me mirroring the politicians, drinking Château Margaux and using gold eating-irons.' The medic gave me Plié's green beret and watched as I put it on, then he adjusted it so the badge was over my left eye. I said, 'Careful they might mistake me for a commando.' He said, 'You are. And on Active Service. You won't need senna.' I said, 'I'm not a marine no more.' He said, 'You can't escape them.' I said, 'You know about him and me, don't you?' The medic said, 'I broke the code when Plié told me that you two were joined at the hip. He got pissed and out came his theory that there is only one person in life that you fall deeply in love with, no matter if you meet a million more people, there is only that one person. Ralph happened to have testicles but Plié fell for Ralph from day one, seduced him with a massage. Plié, never lacking in confidence, said Intelligence approved of you two. On the *Canberra* on the voyage out the women were stampeding to get to Plié and he loved it but the lads still call you the boyfriend. I mean, it shone out of him, for Christ's sakes. And Plié carried that photo of you looking beautiful but dead *in my wallet next to my heart,* he told every fucker.' I said, 'Me doing what ashore? Yomping? I don't think so, I am exhausted after a slow waltz. I volunteered for Intelligence to avoid the green-beret-keeping-fit nutters. And me shooting teenage conscripts? Killing people is wrong.' Reading my paybook, he said, 'Thought so. Your name is Sergei. Sorry, Ralph, that'll stick. And it was you who wiped out the four terrorists. Plié was not the man to hide his light under a bushel. You come across smooth and bristling kudos. You'll survive.' I said, 'Plié has outed me. I'm vulnerable.' He said, 'Balls. The lads'll pull your pisser and that's it.' I said, 'I've never got comfortable with being queer.' He said, 'It'll cheer them up. They'll get to meet the Ruskie boyfriend. You'll be SirGay. Having a laugh is one way of coping with the shit conditions. They loved Plié's bullshit and took the piss. They'll be grieving too 'cos he is one of us. You speak Spanish good and you won't be killing no one. You'll be back on the Frog wine and using a cigarette holder. You could lie and say you speak only pidgin Spanish then you'll be shooting people. Shooting people gets them dead. You know that. Pity the fucking politicians don't. When you see the C.O. get sensible and wear the silk dressing gown and speaka Espagnol.'

"When I told him I would not do that, he took my hand in his, said, 'I'm straight but I've held many men's hands. One Argie with a bad moustache and a doormat of a chest took a fancy to me. I let him down gently. Carrying a stretcher would not be too much of an effort for you?' I said, 'Better than a gun.' He said, 'I'll see the C.O., get you stretcher-bearing with pidgin Spanish as a plus and modelling as a sideline.' As I took off the beret, he said, 'Leave it! Keeps the rain off and the lads will be queuing to see you with clothes on and in costume.' In the cramped noisy helicopter I lifted the lint to look at Plié's face. The medic crossed himself."

Wayland brought me back to reality. "You see death when you jump?"

"Yes, I see him."

"For you tomorrow is Remembrance Day," he said.

I waved at Punk, serious faced, watching me from the far end of the pool.

Scotch finished; finished my Coke too so I took Wayland's Coke and drained it. Got naked. Wayland was looking at me as I stood at the edge of the pool, holding my boxers.

I said, "You okay, lover? Tomorrow fifteen hundred hours? Tandem, you and me. Freefall descent. Speed one hundred m. p. h. for one minute. Then the chute opens."

"I'm scared, Ralph."

"Tell me about it. We'll hold hands." I threw my boxers in his face. "Truth is it's something else. It's best in a plane full of men. It's orderly, powerful and very crazy, like organised insanity… I mean, think about it. A plane full of men who are going to jump out of it? They are silent. Look at their faces. God, it's thrilling. Your first jump is with me… I'm as good as Plié. Might be better than Punk."

He came and stood alongside me at the pool's edge. "Go talk to Punk? He's worried about you."

I dived in, swam underwater, surfaced, and as my crawl is not the best, I did the breaststroke which is for girls according to the treading-on-hands-sergeant. At the far end of the pool, I gently gripped Punk's ankles. "Tomorrow is you with the Aston Martin hunk; me with Wayland."

"I can trust you to get a job done," he said.

"Fingers crossed. Your hair looks good." Punk was

letting his hair grow. It was thick and dark and curling and wonderfully wild even when wet.

"I'm still pug ugly," he said.

"You're not that."

"Race you?"

"I don't do competitive shit." I climbed out the pool.

Punk caught up with me. "The course you done should have been static-line low-level jumps according to Jasper. He reckons you were in a hush-hush outfit. Freefalling at night with oxygen? Jumping from vehicles onto concrete surfaces? Water jumps at night and abseiling from helicopters?" Punk said, as he walked alongside me, "Was it the S.A.S.?"

I pushed my face into his shoulder.

"What's up?" he said.

"Jasper wants to stop reading comic books. Plenty of marines are parachutists. And they do water jumps."

"So it was the commandos?"

"I was a sort of a spasmodic green beret wearer. Complicated. Tell you in Valparaiso." I said, pushing him into the mosaic tiled shower cubicle.

"Tonight," he said, his muscles moving as I soaped his shoulders.

"Valparaiso," I said, soaping his buttocks until he said, "You tell Wayland but you don't tell me?"

The intimacy of the confessional should be between me and Punk not between me and Wayland. I said, "I keep things from you. Like me being a coward."

"That time in the bog you talked smooth but you was terrified about jumping. And on the Sunday when you jumped, Graham saw the cool Ralph but I sees the face on you. I gets to see that face on some jumping. They gets my vote because they are shitting themselves but they jump."

Turning off the shower, he said, "Wayland's pocketed your boxers? That got some esoteric significance?"

"Don't know what esoteric means."

"Ralph, you going off me?"

"My pickup technique used to be to sit back, blow cool smoke, eye up the queue and wait. I raced after you and I would race again, so drop it?"

"Can I…?"

"I am terrified about jumping. I can only cope with one thing at a time. I've got to get Wayland to jump. He is way too close to me and with his gran going he'll be more reliant. But on the course with seven women? He's a lovely kid and he's bound to hook up with one. Give me breathing space and I'll tell you anything but don't rush me."

"You okay?" he said, thumbing the tears streaming down my cheeks.

"The Girl Guides wouldn't have me. My swimming is shit. I am the loser who camouflages his cockups by being tight-lipped. I've even convinced you I was in the S.A.S. I don't want to race no one to prove I am crap 'cos I know I am crap. Wayland is crap. He and me are crap buddies. Don't put me on no pedestal, Punk. My first jump, I had to be pushed. I've never told that to no one, and that includes Plié, but I had to tell Wayland to get him to jump."

"Tomas mentioned you was in the Falklands?"

"Yes, the weather was very disappointing."

"I've been reading about Post Traumatic Stress Disorder in Vietnam," he said.

"You think I have shellshock and you fling me out of a plane?"

"You have to face your bogies and I am supporting you," said Punk.

“Your parents are the social workers not you.”

“Ralph, at times you hurt me.”

With my mouth in Punk’s hair, I said, “Saw a proper doctor who said he thought it was battle shock. Was green-lighted to a specialist who tries to avoid labels and said, ‘who the hell is normal?’ but he reckons I have a problem but I’m lucky ’cos I am curing myself because I have you and I am eating properly again and I had a ‘robust’ upbringing because I had one hell of a mother who was good at liking people, human frailties and all.

“My father was a British diplomat, and when he died the Foreign Office provided for my education so Mum brought me to the UK. She went back to Russia when I joined the marines. She died of cancer on the same day Plié died. Their deaths were my punishment for shooting three men. Three young men having a beer. One bullet apiece – none of Hollywood’s spray-the-bastards drama. Blood. Bit slippery underfoot. One was staggering, then on his knees pleading. The Sten had jammed so he died slow. I keep seeing him again and again, blood slow coming. At night when I can’t sleep.”

Punk was cuddling me. “They were sexy?”

“And how. One guy with no top, muscular shoulders and symmetrical dark body hair – Jesus! I longed to have sex with him, terrorist or no terrorist. I shot him in the chest, thinking that.”

“If they had been old men?”

“The fourth man was middle aged. He shot me with an expression of hurt on his face. Reciprocal bullets in the Wild East, Plié said. Plié would say that. But I reckon it is to do with power: the power of the gun and my misusing it. I see what the Italian psychiatrist was getting at.

“Plié was ordered to kill all four men but he held back

’cos I was in charge. Plié would have arrested them. He deliberately disabled the terrorist guy but action-man me shot the other three. Okay, Plié was a bullshitter but what you saw is what you got. He was beautiful. He was the best. He could shoot a silver dollar out the sky. Plié could think. Plié could rationalise. He knew that our control wanted revenge. That’s why the British had teamed him with me. Common sense Plié would restrain me but I took no notice. And when I fucked up he covered for me. You are a bit like Plié but without the vanity.”

“But you were a British serviceman?”

“Who was given half a house by whom? The British give medals not money.”

“And sex with the older man?” said Punk intuitively.

“It had been on the cards. A man who drank tea with a Kalashnikov on the table. A man who had slaughtered innocents. Chances are he would have killed me after sex. His ejaculation would have been something else. This is why I am seriously flawed. I wouldn’t have said no to sex with him. I disgust myself.”

A bright eyed Wayland greeted Punk. “You sure you want me stopping?”

“You can cook. It’s too late to escape,” said Punk trying for normality; his arm still tight embracing my waist. “I’m starved?”

“Gammon for us; eggs for Ralph.”

I said, “Do you think I am a nut case?” To ask Wayland if I had Post Traumatic Stress Disorder would start a confusion of questions.

“I think you should drive us tomorrow?” said Wayland.

“Where did that come from? Punk? For fuck’s sakes!”

Punk’s grip on my waist was near hurting. I thought, if he says, ‘I am here for you’ I’ll explode but he said, “What you said changes nothing about how I feel about you, Ralph."

"When we get back there are holiday snaps you might care to look at."

"What are you saying?"

"One of me. Naked and dead. Plié took it for the family album."

We dressed in silence.

In the car I said, "Sorry about that shit. Tomorrow is the anniversary of his death."

"Now I feel bad," said Punk.

Wayland said, "Don't worry, Punk, I'll look after Ralph when him and me are in the plane tomorrow."

I giggled. Thank God for Wayland.

"I don't think you should jump tomorrow, Ralph," said Punk, relaxing as he started the Jaguar. "Love this motor."

"Plié's. He might be okay you having it. I wouldn't take bets."

"When I was driving the bus that last day? I was praying I'd meet you again. I had been dreaming of you and me properly together," he said.

He's talking about loyalty to each other and working and living together, I thought.

Like the way Plié and I lived and worked together.

I said, "Tomorrow I'll jump."

LOOKING FOR SOMETHING

IN BRIGHTON

Daily Kevin has been exercising his lovely dog with me in tow after he finishes work.

Kevin is short, with dark-brown thick curling hair, good cheekbones, a faded green striped t-shirt, patched jeans. He is on the right side of twenty-five, though he will kid on that he is only nineteen. His good eyes are full of sadness. His accent is Scottish and that is where he belongs, he tells me. I tell him he belongs with me and Sheba.

The promenade is alive. An important TUC conference. The miners are split. I take interest because the trades union delegates stay in good hotels. I want them lodging in bed and breakfast joints and eating in greasy spoons. Placards every few yards, television crews loiter, stubbing out cigarettes at the entrance to the *Metropole*. Groups of earnest people talk. Kevin is left wing and hates the Tories and thinks the SDP are traitors. And being with him, I want to wave my banner in support while secretly I admire the SDP.

We were in bed an hour ago. It was our last time together and Kevin was apologising for rushing, for not showering first, having worked all day humping furniture and setting up rooms for functions but he wanted to say goodbye properly. Holding me, he told me he would let me keep his dog.

Sheba is in the flat now as Kevin walks Brighton seafront with me for the last time. I grip his arm. His lips tighten as I told him it was a pity he didn't like me as much as I like him.

"I like you more than anyone," he said quietly.

"Why finish it?"

Kevin is going back home because his dad is terminally ill and there is no one to look after him. Kevin will be nurse and run the family business.

"Cheer up, I'll ring you, you know that. Come up on holiday," he said.

Kevin works hard, is respected for it, likes drink a little too much but so do I. We are naturally together, go on holiday together, Spain before discovering Greece. Loved Crete especially, the people, the smaller villages not spoilt by tourists. Being in Crete with him twice last year was so good…

I gave him fifty pounds towards his train fare but he gave it back to me, said he'd ring tomorrow evening. The rain off the sea dampened his face as he put his suitcase in a taxi.

I walked back to my flat for I cannot bear to see him off at the station.

He understands that.

The man who stopped me was a good looking Indian and held a caring umbrella over my head and asked if I would like a leaflet? And perhaps I might come to a meeting on meditation in an hotel around the corner?

"An hotel? Is your English too perfect?"

Big smile. "It's out of the rain. Perhaps calm your

thoughts?" he said, almost knowingly as he led the way.

Yoga. Certainly not the Westernised Yoga for a dabbling Mrs Young-Married bulging in her leotard and desperate to lose twenty pounds, this was serious stuff. How to still the mind, kill thoughts. Ask the Self, Who am I?

I had expected a crowd of getting-old flower-power people in cheesecloth shirts with long hair needing attention but the men and women were well dressed. Kevin, I reflected sadly, would not fit in nor would he want to fit in. On the low stage a man played a sitar redolent of Eastern mysticism and it set the scene for the thirty or more people: a youngish man in worn jeans wearing a *Ban the Bomb* badge, a middle age man who had an Amish style beard as though to advertise his devoutness. The lecturer, an Indian woman, in a clear voice spoke of the inner path to That. And by her side stood an Englishman in his late forties. He was clean cut as was the man who talked to me who had jet black hair with one or two strands of grey; brown eyes and small good hands. He spoke sincerely. The unobservant might mistake his quiet manner for obsequiousness. He had spent time on retreat in a monastery but the answer was not there, he told me, adding,

"It was a community… The people are good… but not what I want. They want to please the bishop, get promotion – that kind of hierarchy. Know what I mean?"

I nodded, knowing exactly what he meant and said, "When the lecturer talks of 'That', she means God?"

"What is God? What is 'That'? Not Who is 'That'? You must seek the answer. 'That' doesn't have genitals, I suspect."

He was teasing me so I said, "Then I am doomed. My

quest is seeking men's genitals."

He was unfazed and mildly amused. "Maybe that search has led you here? Here one gives up things. Are you into abstinence? I am."

I deliberately missed out on the orange juice but took a sticky fudge-like biscuit. The sandwiches, I suspect, were meatless but I wouldn't ask. As I am vegetarian it might seem to be my criticism if they were not.

Before the lecture was a stillness in the room, a stillness that held and lasted – maybe it emanated from the front row: from the elderly man with the long white hair but maybe it came from the powerfully built Indian guy who had picked me up and brought me to hear about meditation. He was as sexy as hell.

The hotel is sprinting distance from the pub. A pub-pub not a poseur's paradise. And I desperately needed a drink. A drink with a man who is thirty-five, he told me, and who asked me if I cared to talk? He was charming. He apologised that he was puddled but did I write poetry?

"Puddled?"

"A polite word for me being as pissed as assholes," he said. There is a scar on his forehead, it strengthens the almost delicate face. It took him awhile to gather his thoughts when I asked him how many pints he had drank?

"Eleven." Then he recited his poetry, his passionate words breaking through the juke box noise. Poets are allowed to do that, read their poetry out loud, I mean. He talked then of his heat exhaustion after he had spent time in Ethiopia where he had held a dead baby boy in his arms. Tear followed tear then another and another. "Six dead babies I held – all boys. Then stopped counting."

His name is Edward. His pale blue eyes were out of focus, it was as if he had left them to their own devices, to get on with it. His longish dark hair was flattened by rain but he doesn't care. I imagined him hatless, coatless, walking slowly, so slowly as if wanting to get drenched. His hands are strong, the nails bitten unlike the fine hands of the man who had been on retreat. I told him of that man.

"I would have liked to have met him, Paul," he said.

"How do you know my name?" I said amazed.

Edward ignored that and asked me how far away I lived but I was unreceptive, he is too drunk.

The other customers in the barn sized barroom seem to be lonely: some worn old things exchange an occasional word, two threadbare queens shrug now and then, a young charmer with a tired walk is not watching us but in reality is watching everyone. All are on watch, waiting for something. When Edward had difficulty downing his beer I thought maybe I should take him to the lavatory, encourage him to vomit.

He left me, shaking my hand. Left me looking at the others distant at the bar, and I regretted Edward leaving. Regretted not embracing him, regretted not having asked the man who had been on retreat to join us to talk.

I should have taken Edward home. He wanted me to. Sick on the carpet? So what? Edward is vulnerable and caring as Kevin is vulnerable and caring. Love Kevin. Lost him though, Kevin is young and attractive and will inevitably find a boyfriend soon, we both know that.

Safe in my pocket was the leaflet with the contact number and address. Meditation.

I banged out the pub door, turned left, caught up with a hurrying Edward, my arm tight in his as I said,

"Please come to my flat to talk?"

The tears were full on. "Hundreds dying in Ethopia."

The shorter of two passing youths shouted at us, "Fancy ten inches?"

"Fuck off," said Edward.

"Later in the week, we'll go meet that man I talked about?" I said.

"Can we, please? Next weekend?" said Edward, leaning on me.

The youths' cackles were growing distant. A feebly shouted: "Ten inches?"

"Edward, you okay?" I said.

"Feel fine now. It's stopped raining."

"Come see my friend's dog? Mine now. Him leaving Sheba with me broke his heart. Left her loving me but she loves him best. That's life. It's still early. You fancy tea and a sandwich?"

"Please. I am a boring vegetarian but cheese or just toast is fine," said Edward.

Arm in arm, we walked home.

Lightning Source UK Ltd.
Milton Keynes UK
UKOW031814070613

211935UK00001B/2/P

9 781904 585428